JOHN KESSEL
ANOTHER ORPHAN

A TOM DOHERTY ASSOCIATES BOOK
NEW YORK

ANOTHER ORPHAN

Copyright © 1982 by John Kessel

A TOR Book
Published by Tom Doherty Associates, Inc.
49 West 24 Street
New York, NY 10010

Cover art by Tom Kidd

ISBN: 0-812-55963-0   Can. ISBN: 0-812-54302-5

First Tor edition: March 1989

Printed in the United States of America

0 9 8 7 6 5 4 3 2 1

IN THE END, EVERYBODY BUT ISHMAEL DIED . . .

He had to get back. Sleep, sleep, you idiot, he told himself. He could not keep from laughing; it welled up in his chest and burst through his tightly closed lips. Fallon's laugh sounded more like a man gasping for breath than one overwhelmed by humor: he barked, he chuckled, he sucked in sudden draughts of air as he tried to control the spasms. Tears were in his eyes, and he twisted his head from side to side as if he were strapped to a bed. Some of the others stirred and cursed him, but Fallon, a character in a book where everyone died on the last page, shook with helpless laughter, crying, knowing he would not sleep.

The Tor Double Novels:

1

"And I only am escaped alone to tell thee."
—*Job*

HE woke to darkness and swaying and the stink of many bodies. He tried to lift his head and reach across the bed and found he was not in his bed at all. He was in a canvas hammock that rocked back and forth in a room of other hammocks.

"Carol?" Still half-asleep, he looked around, then lay back, hoping that he might wake and find this just a dream. He felt the distance from himself he often felt in dreams. But the room did not go away, and the smell of sweat and salt water and some overwhelming stink of oil became more real. The light slanting down through a latticed grating above became brighter; he heard the sound of water and the creak of canvas, and the swaying did not stop, and the men about him began to stir. It came to him, in that same dream-like calm, that he was on a ship.

A bell sounded twice, then twice again. Most of the other men were up, grumbling, and stowing away the hammocks.

"What ails you, Fallon?" someone called. "Up, now."

2

His name was Patrick Fallon. He was thirty-two
years old, a broker for a commission house at the
Chicago Board of Trade. He played squash at an
athletic club every Tuesday and Thursday night. He
lived with a woman named Carol Bukaty.

The night before, he and Carol had gone to a
party thrown by one of the other brokers and his
wife. As sometimes happened with these parties,
this one had degenerated into an exchange of
sexual innuendo, none of it apparently serious, but
with undertones of suspicions and the desire to
hurt. Fallon had had too much wine and had said a
few things to the hostess and about Carol that he
had immediately wanted to retract. They'd driven
back from the party in silence, but the minute
they'd closed the door it had been a fight. Neither
of them shouted, but his quiet statement that he
did not respect her at all and hers that she was
sickened by his excess, managed quite well. They
had become adept at getting at each other. They
had, in the end, made up, and had made love.

As Fallon had lain there on the edge of sleep, he
had had the idle thought that what had happened
that evening was silly, but not funny. That something was wrong.

Fallon had the headache that was the residue of

the wine; he could still smell Carol. He was very hungry and dazed as he stumbled into the bright sunlight on the deck of the ship. It was there. It was real. He was awake. The ocean stretched flat and empty in all directions. The ship rolled slightly as it made way with the help of a light wind, and despite the early morning it was already hot. He did not hear the sound or feel the vibration of an engine. Fallon stared, unable to collect the scattered impressions into coherence; they were all consistent with the picture of an antiquated sailing ship on a very real ocean, all insane when compared with where his mind told him he ought to be.

The men had gone to their work as soon as they'd stretched into the morning light. They wore drab shirts and canvas trousers; most were barefoot. Fallon walked unsteadily along the deck, trying to keep out of their way as they set to scrubbing the deck. The ship was unlike anything he had ever seen on Lake Michigan; he tried to ignore the salt smell that threatened to make it impossible for him to convince himself this was Lake Michigan. Yet it seemed absurd for such a small vessel to be in the middle of an ocean. He knew that the Coast Guard kept sailing ships for training its cadets, but these were no cadets.

The deck was worn, scarred and greasy with a kind of oily, clear lard-like grease. The rail around the deck was varnished black and weather-beaten, but the pins set through it to which the rigging was secured were ivory. Fallon touched one—it was some kind of tooth. More ivory was used for rigging-blocks and on the capstan around which the anchor chain was wound. The ship was a thing of black wood fading to white under the assault of water and sun, and of white ivory corroding to black under the effect of dirt and hard use. Three long boats, pointed at both ends, hung from arms of wood and metal on the left—the port—side; another such boat was slung at the rear of the deck on the starboard side, and on the raised part of the deck behind the mainmast two other boats were turned turtle and secured. Add to this the large hatch on the main deck and a massive brick structure that looked like some old-fashioned oven just behind the front mast, and there hardly seemed room for the fifteen or twenty men on deck to go about their business. There was certainly no place to hide.

"Fallon! Set your elbows to that deck or I shall have to set your nose to it!" A short, sandy-haired man accosted him. Stocky and muscular, he was some authority; there was insolence in his grin, and some seriousness. The other men looked up.

Fallon got out of the man's way. He went over to one of the groups washing down the deck with salt water, large scrub brushes, and what looked like push brooms with leather flaps instead of bristles, like large versions of the squeegees used to clean windows. The sandy-haired man watched him as he got down on his hands and knees and grabbed one of the brushes.

"There's a good lad, now. Ain't he, fellows?"

A couple of them laughed. Fallon started scrubbing, concentrating on the grain of the wood, at first fastidious about not wetting the already damp trousers he had apparently slept in, soon realizing that that was a lost cause. The warm water was sloshed over them, the men leaned on the brushes, and the oil slowly flaked up and away through the spaces in the rail into the sea. The sun rose and it became even hotter. Now and then one of the men tried to say a word or two to him, but he did not answer.

"Fallon here's got the hypos," someone said.

"Or the cholera," another said. "He does look a bit bleary about the eye. Are you thirsty, Fallon? D'your legs ache? Are your bowels knotted?"

"My bowels are fine," he said.

That brought a good laugh. "Fine, he says! Manx-man!" The sailor called to a decrepit old man leaning on his squeegee. "Tell the King-Post that Fallon's bowels are fine, now! The scrubbing does seem to have eased them."

"Don't ease them here, man!" the old man said seriously. The men roared again, and the next bucket of water was sloshed up between Fallon's legs.

3

In the movies men had faced similar situations. The amnesiac soldier came to on a farm in Wales. But invariably the soldier would give evidence of his confusion, challenging the farm owner, pestering his fellow workers with questions about where he was and how he got there, telling them of his persistent memory of a woman in white with golden hair. Strangely—strangely even to Fallon—he did not feel that way. Confusion, yes, dread, curiosity—but no desire to call attention to himself, to try to make the obvious reality of his situation give way to the apparent reality of his memories. He did not think this was because of any strength of character or remarkable powers of adaptation. In fact, everything he did that first day revealed his ignorance of what he was supposed to know and do on the ship. He did not feel any great presence of mind; for minutes at a time he would stop working, stunned with awe and fear at the simple alienness of what was happening. If it was a dream, it was a vivid dream. If anything was a dream, it was Carol and the Chicago Board of Trade.

The soldier in the movie always managed, despite the impediments of his amnesia and the ignorance of those around him, to find the rational answer to his mystery. That shell fragment which had grazed his forehead in Normandy had sent him back to a Wessex sanitorium, from which he had wandered during an air raid, to be picked up by a local handyman driving his lorry to Llanelly, who in the course of the journey decided to turn a few quid by leasing the poor soldier to a farmer as his half-wit cousin laborer. So it had to be that some physicist at the University of Chicago, working on the modern equivalent of the Manhattan Project, had accidentally created a field of gravitational energy so intense that a vagrant vortex had broken free from it, and, in its lightning progress through the city on its way to extinction, had plucked Fallon from his bed in the suburbs, sucked him through a puncture in the fabric of space and time, to deposit him in a hammock on a mid-nineteenth-century sailing ship. Of course.

Fallon made a fool of himself ten times over

during the day. Despite his small experience with
fresh-water sailing, he knew next to nothing about
the work he was meant to do on this ship. Besides
cleaning the deck and equipment, the men
scrubbed a hard, black soot from the rigging and
spars. Fallon would not go up into the rigging. He
was afraid, and tried to find work enough on the
deck. He did not ask where the oil and soot had
come from; it was obvious the source had been the
brick furnace that was now topped by a tight-fitting
wooden cover. Some of the cracks in the deck were
filled with what looked like dried blood, but it was
only the casual remark of one of the other men that
caused him to realize, shocked at his own slow-
ness, that this was a whaling ship.

The crew was an odd mixture of types and races;
there were white and black, a group of six Orientals who sat apart on the rear deck and took no
part in the work, men with British and German
accents, and an eclectic collection of others—
Polynesians, an Indian, a huge, shaven-headed
black African, and a mostly naked man covered
from head to toe with purple tattoos, whorls and
swirls and vortexes, images and symbols, none of
them quite decipherable as a familiar object or
person. After the decks had been scrubbed to a
remarkable whiteness, the mate named Flask set
Fallon to tarring some heavy ropes in the fore part
of the ship, by himself, where he would be out of
the others' way. The men seemed to realize that
something was wrong with him, but said nothing
and apparently did not take it amiss that one of
their number should begin acting strangely.

Which brought him, hands and wrists smeared
with warm tar, to the next question: how did they

know who he was? He was Fallon to all of them. He had obviously been there before he awakened; he had been a regular member of the crew with a personality and role to fill. He knew nothing of that. He had the overwhelming desire to get hold of a mirror to see whether the face he wore was indeed the face he had worn in Chicago the night before. The body was the same, down to the appendix scar he'd carried since he was nine years old. His arms and hands were the same; the fatigue he felt and the rawness of his skin told him he had not been doing this type of work long. So assume he was there in his own person, his Chicago person, the *real* Fallon. Was there now some confused nineteenth-century sailor wandering around a brokerage house on Van Buren? The thought made him smile. The sailor at the Board of Trade would probably get the worst of it.

So they knew who he was, even if he didn't remember ever having been here before. There was a Patrick Fallon on the ship, and *he* had somehow been brought here to fill that role. Reasons unknown. Method unknown. Way out . . .

Think of it as an adventure. How many times as a boy had he dreamed of similar escapes from the mundane? Here he was, the answer to a dream, twenty-five years later. It would make a tremendous story when he got back, if he could find someone he could trust enough to tell it to—if he could get back.

There was a possibility that he tried to keep himself from dwelling on. He had come here while asleep, and though this reality gave no evidence of being a dream, if there was a symmetry to insanity, then on waking the next morning, might he not be back in his familiar bed? Logic presented the possibility. He tried not to put too much faith in logic. Logic had not helped him when he was on the wrong side of the soybean market in December, 1980.

The long tropic day declined; the sunset was a travel agent's dream. They were traveling east, by the signpost of that light. Fallon waited, sitting by a coil of rope, watching the helmsman at the far end of the ship lean, dozing, on the long ivory tiller that served this ship in place of the wheel with handspikes he was familiar with from Errol Flynn movies. It had to be a bone from some long-dispatched whale, another example of the savage Yankee practicality of whoever had made this whaler. It was a queerly innocent, gruesome artistry. Fallon had watched several idle sailors in the afternoon carving pieces of bone while they ate their scrap of salt pork and hard bread.

"Fallon, you can't sleep out here tonight, unless you want the Old Man to find you lying about." It was a tall sailor of about Fallon's age. He had come down from aloft shortly after Fallon's assignment to the tar bucket, had watched him quietly for some minutes before giving him a few pointers on how the work was done. In the falling darkness, Fallon could not make out his expression, but the voice held a quiet distance that might mask just a trace of kindness. Fallon tried to get up and found his legs had grown so stiff he failed on the first try. The sailor caught his arm and helped him to his feet. "You're all right?"

"Yes." Fallon was embarrassed.

"Let's get below, then." They stepped toward the latticed hatch near the bow.

"And there he is," the sailor said, pausing, lifting his chin aft.

"Who?" Fallon looked back with him and saw the black figure there, heavily bearded, tall, in a long coat, steadying himself by a hand in the rigging. The oil lamp above the compass slightly illuminated the dark face—and gleamed deathly white along the ivory leg that projected from beneath his black coat. Fixed, immovable, the man leaned heavily on it.

"Ahab," the sailor said.

4

Lying in the hammock, trying to sleep, Fallon was assaulted by the feverish reality of where he was. The ship rocked him like a gentle parent in its progress through the calm sea; he heard the rush of water breaking against the hull as the *Pequod* made headway, the sighing of the breeze above, heard the steps of the nightwatch on deck, the occasional snap of canvas, the creaking of braces; he sweated in the oppressive heat below-decks; he drew heavy breaths, trying to calm himself, of air laden with the smell of mildewed canvas and what he knew to be whale oil. He held his hands before his face and in the profound darkness knew them to be his own. He touched his neck and felt the slickness of sweat beneath the beard. He ran his tongue over his lips and tasted salt. Through the open hatch he could make out stars that were unchallenged by any other light. Would the stars be the same in a book as they were in reality?

In a book. Any chance he had to sleep flew from him whenever he ran up against that thought. Any logic he brought to bear on his situation crumbled under the weight of that absurdity. A time machine he could accept, some chance cosmic displacement that sucked him into the past. But not into a book. That was insanity; that was hallucination. He knew that if he could sleep now, he would wake once more in the real world. But he had nothing to grab hold of. He lay in the darkness listening to the ship and could not sleep at all.

They had been compelled to read *Moby Dick* in the junior-year American Renaissance class he'd taken to fulfill the last of his Humanities requirements. Fallon remembered being bored to tears by most of Melville's book, struggling with his interminable sentences, his woolly speculations that had no bearing on the story; he remembered being caught up by parts of that story. He had seen the movie with Gregory Peck. Richard Basehart, king of the sci-fi flicks, had played Ishmael. Fallon had not seen anyone who looked like Richard Basehart on this ship. The mate, Flask—he remembered that name now. He remembered that all the harpooners were savages. Queequeg.

He remembered that in the end, everyone but Ishmael died.

He had to get back. Sleep, sleep, you idiot, he told himself. He could not keep from laughing; it welled up in his chest and burst through his tightly

closed lips. Fallon's laugh sounded more like a
man gasping for breath than one overwhelmed by
humor: he barked, he chuckled, he sucked in
sudden draughts of air as he tried to control the
spasms. Tears were in his eyes, and he twisted his
head from side to side as if he were strapped to a
bed in some ward. Some of the others stirred and
cursed him, but Fallon, a character in a book
where everyone died on the last page, shook with
helpless laughter, crying, knowing he would not
sleep.

5

With a preternatural clarity born of the sleepless
night, Fallon saw the deck of the *Pequod* the next
morning. He was a little stunned yet, but if he kept
his mind in tight check the fatigue would keep him
from thinking, and he would not feel the distress
that was waiting to burst out again. Like a man
carrying a bowl filled with acid, Fallon carried his
knowledge tenderly.

He observed with scientific detachment, knowing that sleep would ultimately come, and with it
perhaps escape. The day was bright and fair, a
duplicate of the previous one. The whaler was
clean and prepared for her work; all sails were set
to take advantage of the light breeze, and the

mastheads were manned with lookouts. Men loi-
tered on deck. On the rear deck—the quarter-
deck, they called it—Ahab paced, with remarkable
steadiness for a man wearing an ivory leg, between
the compass in its box and the mainmast, stopping
for seconds to stare pointedly at each end of his
path. Fallon could not take his eyes off the man. He
was much older than Fallon had imagined him
from his memories of the book. Ahab's hair and
beard were still black, except for the streak of
white which ran through them as the old scar ran
top to bottom across his face, but the face itself was
deeply worn, and the man's eyes were sunken in
wrinkles, hollow. Fallon remembered Tigue who
had traded in the gold pit, who had once been the
best boy on the floor—the burn-out, they called
him now, talking a very good game about shorting
the market. Tigue's eyes had the same hollow
expectation of disaster waiting inevitably for him
—just him—that Ahab's held. Yet when Fallon had
decided Ahab had to be the same empty nonentity,
the man would pause at the end of his pathway and
stare at the compass, or the gold coin that was
nailed to the mast, and his figure would tighten in
the grip of some stiffening passion, as if he were
shot through with lightning. As if he were at the
focal point of some cosmic lens that concentrated
all the power of the sun on him, so that he might
momentarily burst into spontaneous flame.

Ahab talked to himself, staring at the coin. His
voice was conversational, and higher pitched than
Fallon had imagined it would be. Fallon was not
the only man who watched him in wonder and
fear.

"There's something ever egotistical in moun-

tain-tops and towers, and all other grand and lofty
things; look here—three peaks as proud as Lucifer.
The firm tower, that is Ahab; the volcano, that is
Ahab; the courageous, the undaunted, and victori-
ous fowl, that, too, is Ahab; all are Ahab; and this
round globe is but the image of the rounder globe,
which, like a magician's glass, to each and every
man in turn but mirrors back his own mysterious
self . . ."

All spoken in the tone of a man describing a
minor auto accident (the brown Buick swerved to
avoid the boy on the bicycle, crossed over the
yellow line and hit the milk truck which was going
south on Main Street). As soon as he had stopped,
Ahab turned and, instead of continuing his pacing,
went quietly below.

One of the ship's officers—the first mate, Fallon
thought—who had been talking to the helmsman
before Ahab began to speak, now advanced to look
at the coin. Fallon began to remember what was
going to happen. Theatrically, though there was
nobody there to listen to him, the mate began to
speak aloud about the Trinity and the sun, hope
and despair. Next came another mate, who talked
of spending it quickly, then gave a reading compar-
ing the signs of the zodiac to a man's life. Overwrit-
ten and silly, Fallon thought.

Flask now came to the doubloon and figured out
how many cigars he could buy with it. Then came
the old man who had sloshed the water all over
Fallon the previous morning, who gave a reading of
the ship's doom under the sign of the lion. Then
Queequeg, then one of the Orientals, then a black
boy—the cabin boy.

The boy danced around the mast twice, crouching low, rising on his toes, and each time around stared at the doubloon with comically bugged eyes. He stopped. "I look, you look, he looks, we look, ye look, they look."

I look, you look, he looks, we look, ye look, they look.

They all looked at it; they all spouted their interpretations. That was what Melville had wanted them to do to prove his point. Fallon did not feel like trying to figure out what that point was. After the dramatics, the *Pequod* went back to dull routine, and he to clean up work on the deck, to tarring more ropes. They had a lot of ropes.

He took a break and walked up to the mast to look at the coin himself. Its surface was stamped with the image of three mountains, with a flame, a tower, and a rooster at their peaks. Above were the sun and the signs of the zodiac. REPUBLICA DEL EQUADOR: QUITO, it said. A couple of ounces, worth maybe $1,300 on the current gold market, according to the London fix Fallon last remembered. It wouldn't be worth as much to these men, of course; this was pre-inflation money. He remembered that the doubloon had been nailed there by Ahab as a reward to whoever spotted Moby Dick first.

I look, you look, he looks, we look, ye look, they look.

Fallon looked, and nothing changed. His tiredness grew as the day wore through a brutally hot afternoon. When evening at last came and the grumbling of his belly had been at least partially assuaged by the meager meal served the men, Fallon fell exhausted into the hammock. He did not worry about not sleeping this time; consciousness

fell away as if he had been drugged. He had a vivid
dream. He was trying, under cover of darkness, to
pry the doubloon away from the mast so that he
might throw it into the sea. Anxiously trying not to
let the helmsman at the tiller spot him, he heard
the step, tap, step, tap of Ahab's pacing a deck
below. It was one of those dreams where one
struggles in unfocused terror to accomplish some
simple task. He was afraid he might be found any
second by Ahab. If he were caught, then he would
be exposed and vilified before the crew's indiffer-
ent gaze.

He couldn't do it. He couldn't get his fingers
under the edge of the coin, though he bruised them
bloody. He heard the knocking of Ahab's whalebone step ascending to the deck; the world con-
tracted to the coin welded to the mast, his broken
nails, the terrible fear. He heard the footsteps
drawing nearer behind him as he frantically tried
to free the doubloon, yet he could not run, and he
would not turn around. At the last, after an eternity
of anxiety, a hand fell on his shoulder and spun
him around, his heart leaping into his throat. It
was not Ahab, but Carol.

He woke breathing hard, pulse pounding. He
was still in the hammock, in the forecastle of the
Pequod. He closed his eyes again, dozed fretfully
through the rest of the night. Morning came: he
was still there.

The next day several of the other men prodded
him about not having taken a turn at the masthead
for a long time. He stuck to mumbled answers and
hoped they would not go to any of the officers. He
wanted to disappear. He wanted it to be over. The
men treated him more scornfully as the days
passed. And the days passed, and still nothing

happened to free him. The doubloon glinted in the sun each morning, the center of the ship, and Fallon could not get away. I look, you look, he looks, we look, ye look, they look.

6

Fallon had assumed his sullen station by the tar bucket. There he felt at least some defense from his confusion. He could concentrate on the smell and feel of the tar; he remembered the summers on the tarred road in front of his grandparents' house in Elmira, how the sun would raise shining bubbles of tar at the edges of the re-surfaced country road, how the tar would stick to your sneakers and get you a licking if you tracked it into grandmother's immaculate kitchen. He and his cousin Seth had broken the bubbles with sticks and watched them slowly subside into themselves. The tar bucket on the *Pequod* was something Fallon could focus on. The tar was real; the air he breathed was real— Fallon himself was real.

Stubb, the second mate, stood in front of him, arms akimbo. He stared at Fallon; Fallon lifted his head and saw the man's small smile. There was no charity in it.

"Time to go aloft, Fallon. You've been missing your turn, and we won't have any slackers aboard."

Fallon couldn't think of anything to say. He

stumbled to his feet, wiping his hands on a piece of burlap. A couple of the other sailors were watching, waiting for Fallon to shy off or for Stubb to take him.

"Up with ye!" Stubb shoved Fallon's shoulder, and he turned, fumbling for the rigging. Fallon looked momentarily over the side of the ship to the sea that slid calmly by them; the gentle rolling of the deck that he had in so short a time become accustomed to now returned to him with frightening force. Stubb was still behind him. Taking a good breath, he pulled himself up and stepped barefoot onto the rail. Facing inward now, he tried to climb the rigging. Stubb watched him with dispassion, waiting, it seemed, for his failure. Expecting it. It was like trying to climb one of those rope ladders at the county fair: each rung he took twisted the ladder in the direction of his weight, and the rocking of the ship, magnified as he went higher, made it hard for his feet to find the next step. He had never been a particularly self-conscious man, but felt he was being watched by them all now, and was acutely conscious of how strange he must seem. How touched with idiocy and fear.

Nausea rose, the deck seemed farther below than it had any reason to be, the air was stifling, the wind was without freshness and did not cool the sweat from his brow and neck. He clutched the ropes desperately; he tried to take another step, but the strength seemed drained from his legs. Humiliated, burning with shame yet at the same time mortally afraid of falling—and of more than that, of the whole thing, of the fact that here he was where he ought not to be, cheated, abused, mystified—he wrapped his arms around the rigging, knees wobbly, sickness in his gut, bile threatening to heave itself up the back of his throat. Crying, eyes clenched tight, he wished it would all go away.

"Fallon! Fallon, you dog, you dog-*fish*, why don't you climb! You had better climb, weak-liver, for I don't want you down on my deck again if you won't!" Stubb roared his rage. Fallon opened his eyes, saw the red-faced man staring furiously up at him. Perhaps he'll have a stroke, Fallon thought.

He hung there, half-up, half-down, unable to move. I want to go home, he thought. Let me go home. Stubb raged and ridiculed him; others gathered to laugh and watch. Fallon closed his eyes and tried to go away. He heard a sound like the wooden mallet of the carpenter.

"What is the problem here, Mr. Stubb?" A calm voice. Fallon looked down again. Ahab stood with his hand on the mainmast to steady himself, looking up. His thumb was touching the doubloon.

Stubb was taken by surprise, as if Ahab were some apparition that had been called up by an entirely inappropriate spell. He jerked his head upward to indicate Fallon.

Squinting against the sun, Ahab studied Fallon for some time. His face was unnaturally pale in comparison to the tanned faces of the others turned up to look at him. Yet against the pallor, the white scar ran, a death-like sign, down the side of his face. His dark hair was disarrayed in the hot breeze. He was an old man; he swayed in the attempt to steady himself.

"Why don't ye go up?" Ahab called to Fallon.

Fallon shook his head. He tried to step up

another rung, but though his foot found the rope, he didn't seem to have the strength he needed to pull himself up.

Ahab continued to look at him. He did not seem impatient or angry, only curious, as if Fallon were an animal sitting frozen on a traffic mall, afraid of the cars that passed. He seemed content to stand watching Fallon indefinitely. Stubb shifted nervously from foot to foot, his anger displaced and negated. The crewmen simply watched. Some of them looked above Fallon in the rigging; the ropes he clung to jerked, and he looked up himself to see that the man who had been standing at the masthead was coming down to help him.

"Bulkington!" Ahab cried, waving to the man to stop, "Let him be!" The sailor retreated upward and swung himself onto the yardarm above the mainsail. The *Pequod* waited. If there were whales to be hunted, they waited too.

Very distinctly, so that Fallon heard every word, Ahab said, "You must go up. You have taken the vow with the rest, and I will not have you go back on it. Would you go back on it? You must go up, or else you must come down, and show yourself for the coward and weakling you would then be."

Fallon clung to the rigging. He had taken no vow. It was all a story. What difference did it make what he did in a story? If he was to be a character in a book, why couldn't he defy it, do what he wanted instead of following the path they indicated? By coming down he could show himself as himself.

"Have faith!" Ahab called.

Above him, Bulkington hawked and spat, timing it so that with the wind and the rocking of the *Pequod*, he hit the sea and not the deck. Fallon bent his head back and looked up at him. It was the kind sailor who had helped him below on that first night. He hung suspended. He looked down and watched Ahab sway with the rolling of the deck, his eyes still fixed on Fallon. The man was crazy. Melville was crazy for inventing him.

Fallon clenched his teeth, pulled on the ropes and pushed himself up another step toward the masthead. He was midway up the mainsail, thirty feet above the deck. He concentrated on one rung at a time, breathing steadily, and pulled himself up. When he reached the level of the mainyard, Bulkington swung himself below Fallon and helped him along. The complicated motion that came when the sailor stepped onto the ropes had Fallon clinging once again, but this time he was out of it fairly quickly. They ascended, step by dizzying step, to the masthead. The sailor got onto the port masthead hoop, helping Fallon into the starboard. The *Pequod*'s flag snapped in the wind a couple of feet above their heads.

"And here we are, Fallon," Bulkington said. Immediately he dropped himself down into the rigging again, so nimbly and suddenly that Fallon's breath was stopped in fear for the man's fall.

Way below, the men were once more stirring. Ahab exchanged some words with Stubb; then, moving out to the rail and steadying himself by a hand on one of the stays, a foreshortened black puppet far below, he turned his white face up to Fallon once again. Cupping his hand to his mouth, he shouted, "Keep a steady eye, now! If ye see fin or flank of him, call away!"

Call away. Fallon was far above it all now, alone. He had made it. He had taken no vow and was not obligated to do anything he did not wish to. He had ascended to the masthead of his own free will, but,

if he was to become a whaler, then what harm
would there be in calling out whales—normal
whales? Not literary ones. Not white ones.

He looked out to the horizon. The sea stretched
out to the utmost ends of the world, covering it all,
every secret, clear and blue and a little choppy
under the innocent sky.

7

Fallon became used to the smell of the *Pequod*.
He became accustomed to feeling sweaty and
dirty, to the musty smell of mildew and the tang of
brine trying to push away the stench of the packing
plant.

He had not always been fastidious in his other
life. In the late sixties, after he had dropped out of
Northwestern, he had lived in an old house in a
rundown neighborhood with three other men and
a woman. They had called it "The Big House," and
to the outside observer they must have been hip-
pies. "Hair men." "Freaks." "Dropouts." It was a
vocabulary that seemed quaint now. The perpetual
pile of dirty dishes in the sink, the Fillmore West
posters, the black light, the hot and cold running
roaches, the early-fifties furniture with corners
shredded to tatters by the three cats. Fallon realized that that life had been as different from his

world at the Board of Trade as the deck of the *Pequod* was now.

Fallon had dropped out because, he'd told himself, there was nothing he wanted from the university that he couldn't get from its library, or by hanging around the student union. It was hard for him to believe how much he had read then: Skinner's behaviorism, Spengler's history, pop physics and Thomas Kuhn, Friedman and Galbraith, Shaw, Conrad, Nabokov, and all he could find of Hammett, Chandler, Macdonald and their imitators. Later he had not been able to figure out just why he had forsaken a degree so easily; he didn't know if he was too irresponsible to do the work, or too slow, or above it all and following his own path. Certainly he had not seen himself as a rebel, and the revolutionary fervor his peers affected (it had seemed affectation ninety percent of the time) never took hold of Fallon completely. He had observed, but not taken part in, the melee at the Democratic Convention. But he put in his time in the back bedroom listening to the Doors and blowing dope until the world seemed no more than a slightly bigger version of the Big House and his circle of friends. He read *The Way of Zen*. He knew Hesse and Kerouac. He hated Richard Nixon and laughed at Spiro Agnew. Aloft in the rigging of the *Pequod*, those years came back to Fallon as they never had in his last five years at the CBT. What a different person he had been at twenty. What a strange person, he realized, he had become at twenty-eight. What a marvelous—and frightening —metamorphosis.

He had gotten sick of stagnating, he told himself. He had seen one or another of his friends smoke himself into passivity. He had seen through the self-delusions of the other cripples in the Big House: cripples was what he had called them when he'd had the argument with Marty Solokov and had stalked out. Because he broke from that way of living did not mean he was selling out, he'd told them. He could work any kind of job; he didn't want money or a house in the suburbs. He had wanted to give himself the feeling of getting started again, of moving, of putting meaning to each day. He had quit washing dishes for the university, moved into a dingy flat closer to the center of the city, and scanned the help-wanted columns. He still saw his friends often and got stoned maybe not quite so often, and listened to music and read. But he had had enough of "finding himself," and he recognized in the others how finding yourself became an excuse for doing nothing.

Marty's cousin was a runner for Pearson Joel Chones on the Chicago Mercantile Exchange who had occasionally come by the house, gotten high and gone to concerts. Fallon had slept with her once. He called her up, and she asked around, and eventually he cut his hair short—not too short—and became a runner for Pearson, too. He became marginally better groomed. He took a shower and changed his underwear every day. He bought three ties and wore one of them on the trading floor because that was one of the rules of the exchange.

It occurred to Fallon to find Ishmael, if only to see the man who would live while he died. He listened and watched; he learned the name of every man on the ship—he knew Flask and Stubb and Starbuck and Bulkington, Tashtego, Dagoo and Queequeg, identified Fedallah, the lead Philip-

pine boatsman. There *was* no Ishmael. At first
Fallon was puzzled, then came the beginnings of
hope. If the reality he was living in could be found
to differ from the reality of Melville's book in such
an important particular, then could it not differ in
some other way—some way that would at least
lead to his survival? Maybe this Ahab caught his
white whale. Maybe Starbuck would steel himself
to the point where he could defy the madman and
take over the ship. Perhaps they would never sight
Moby Dick.

Then an unsettling realization smothered the
hope before it could come fully to bloom: there
was not necessarily an Ishmael in the book. "*Call
me Ishmael*," it started. Ishmael was a pseudonym
for some other man, and there would be no one by
that name on the *Pequod*. Fallon congratulated
himself on a clever bit of literary detective work.

Yet the hope refused to remain dead. Yes, there
was no Ishmael on the *Pequod;* or anyone on the
ship not specifically named in the book might be
Ishmael, any one of the anonymous sailors, within
certain broad parameters of age and character—
and Fallon wracked his brain trying to remember
what the narrator said of himself—might be Ishmael. He grabbed at that; he breathed in the
possibility and tried on the suit for size. Why not? If
absurdity were to rule to the extent that he had to
be there in the first place, then why couldn't he be
the one who lived? More than that, why couldn't he
make himself that man? No one else knew what
Fallon knew. He had the advantage over them. Do
the things that Ishmael did, and you may be him. If
you have to be a character in a book, why not be
the hero?

* * *

Fallon's first contact with the heart of capitalism at the CME had been frightening and amusing. Frightening when he screwed up and delivered a May buy-order to a July trader and cost the company 10,000 dollars. It was only through the grace of God and his own guts in facing it out that he had made it through the disaster. He had, he discovered, the ability to hide himself behind a facade which, to the self-interested observer, would appear to be whatever that observer wished it to be. If his superior expected him to be respectful and curious, then Fallon was respectfully curious. He did it without having to compromise his inner self. He was not a hypocrite.

The amusing part came after he had it all down and he began to watch the market like an observer at a very complex monopoly game. Or, more accurately, like a baseball fan during a pennant race. There were at least as many statistics as in a good baseball season, enough personalities, strategies, great plays, blunders, risk and luck. Fallon would walk onto the floor at the beginning of the day—the huge room with its concert-hall atmosphere, the banks of price boards around the walls, the twilight, the conditioned air, the hundreds of bright-coated traders and agents—and think of half time at homecoming. The floor at the end of the day, as he walked across the hardwood scattered with mounds of paper scraps like so much confetti, was a basketball court after the NCAA finals. Topping it all off, giving it that last significant twist that was necessary to all good jokes, was the fact that this was all supposed to mean something; it was real money they were playing with, and one tick of the board in Treasury Bills cost somebody eleven-hundred dollars. This was serious stuff, kid.

The lifeblood of the nation—of the free world.
Fallon could hardly hold in his laughter, could not
stop his fascination.

Fallon's first contact with the whale—his first
lowering—was in Stubb's boat. The man at the
forward masthead cried out, "There she blows!
Three points off starboard! There she blows! Three
—no, four of 'em!"
The men sprang to the longboats and swung
them away over the side. Fallon did his best to look
as if he was helping. Stubb's crew leapt into the
boat as it was dropped into the swelling sea,
heedless to the possibility of broken bones or
sprained ankles. Fallon hesitated a second at the
rail, then threw himself off with the feeling of a
man leaping off the World Trade Center. He landed
clumsily and half-bowled over one of the men. He
took his place at a center oar and pulled away. Like
the man falling off the building, counting off the
stories as they flew past him, Fallon thought, "So
far, so good." And waited for the crash.
"Stop snoring, ye sleepers, and pull!" Stubb
called, halfway between jest and anger. "Pull,
Fallon! Why don't you pull? Have you never seen an
oar before? Don't look over your shoulder, lad,
pull! That's better. Don't be in a hurry, men—
softly, softly now—but damn ye, pull until you
break something! Tashtego! Can't you harpoon me
some men with backs to them? *Pull!*"
Fallon pulled until he thought the muscles in his
arms would snap, until the small of his back
spasmed as if he were indeed being harpooned by
the black-haired Indian behind him in the bow.
The sea was rough, and they were soon soaked
with spray. After a few minutes Fallon forgot the

whales they pursued, merged into the rhythm of
the work, fell in with the cunning flow of Stubb's
curses and pleas, the crazy sermon, now whispered, now shouted. He concentrated on the oar in
his hands, the bite of the blade into the water, the
simple mechanism his body had become, the
working of his lungs, the dry rawness of the breath
dragged in and out in time to their rocking, back-
breaking work. Fallon closed his eyes, heard the
pulse in his ears, felt the cool spray and the hot sun,
saw the rose fog of the blood in his eyelids as he
faced into the bright and brutal day.

At twenty-five, Fallon was offered a position in
the office upstairs. At twenty-seven, he had an offer
from DCB International to become a broker. By
that time he was living with Carol. Why not? He
was still outside it all, still safe within. Let them
think what they would of him; he was protected, in
the final analysis, by that great indifference he held
to his breast the way he held Carol close at night.
He was not a hypocrite. He said nothing he did not
believe in. Let them project upon him whatever
fantasies they might hold dear to themselves. He
was outside and above it all, analyzing futures for
DCB International. Clearly, in every contract that
crossed his desk, it was stated that DCB and its
brokers were not responsible for reverses that
might be suffered as a result of suggestions they
made.
So he had spent the next four years, apart from
it, pursuing his interests, which, with the money he
was making, he found were many. Fallon saw very
little of the old friends now. Solokov's cousin told
him he was now in New York, cadging money from
strangers in Times Square. Solokov, she said,

claimed it was a pretty good living. He claimed he was still beating the system. Fallon had grown up enough to realize that no one really beat any system—as if there were a system. There was only buying and selling, subject to the forces of the market and the infirmities of the players. Fallon was on the edges of it, could watch quietly, taking part as necessary (he had to eat), but still stay safe. He was no hypocrite.

"To the devil with ye, boys, will ye be outdone by Ahab's heathens? Pull, spring it, my children, my fine hearts-alive, smoothly, smoothly, bend it hard starboard! Aye, Fallon, let me see you sweat, lad, can you sweat for me?"

They rose on the swell, and it was like rowing uphill; they slid down the other side, still rowing, whooping like children on a tobaggan ride, all the time Stubb calling on them. Fallon saw Starbuck's boat off to his right; he heard the rush of water beneath them, and the rush of something faster and greater than their boat.

Tashtego grunted behind him.

"A hit, a hit!" Stubb shouted, and beside Fallon the whaleline was running out with such speed that it sang and hummed and smoked. One of the men sloshed water over the place where it slid taut as a wire over the gunnel. Then the boat jerked forward so suddenly that Fallon was nearly knocked overboard when his oar, still trailing in the water, slammed into his chest. Gasping at the pain, he managed to get the oar up into the air. Stubb had half-risen from his seat in the stern.

They flew through the water. The whaleboat bucked as it slapped the surface of every swell the whale pulled them through. Fallon held on for dear life, not sure whether he ought to be grateful he hadn't been pitched out when the ride began. He tried to twist around to see the monster that was towing them, but able to turn only half way, all he could see for the spray and the violent motion was the swell and rush of white water ahead of them. Tashtego, crouched in the bow, grinned wickedly as he tossed out wooden blocks tied to the whaleline in order to tire the whale with their drag. You might as well try to tire a road grader.

Yet he could not help but feel exhilarated, and he saw that the others in the boat, hanging on or trying to draw the line in, were flushed and breathing as hard as he.

He turned again and saw the whale.

Fallon had been a good swimmer in high school. He met Carol Bukaty at a swimming pool about a year after he had gone to work at the CME. Fallon first noticed her in the pool, swimming laps. She was the best swimmer there, better than he, though he might have been stronger than she in the short run. She gave herself over to the water and did not fight it; the kick of her long legs was steady and strong. She breathed easily and her strokes were relaxed, yet powerful. She did not swim for speed, but she looked as if she could swim for days, so comfortable did she seem in the water. Fallon sat on the steps at the pool's edge and watched her for half an hour without once getting bored. He found her grace in the water arousing. He knew he had to speak to her. He slid into the pool and swam laps behind her.

At last she stopped. Holding onto the trough at the end of the pool, she pushed her goggles up onto

her forehead and brushed the wet brown hair away
from her eyes. He drew up beside her.

"You swim very well," he said.

She was out of breath. "Thank you."

"You look as if you wouldn't ever need to come
out of the water. Like anything else might be a
comedown after swimming." It was a strange thing
for him to say, it was not what he wanted to say, but
he did not know what he wanted, besides her.

She looked puzzled, smiled briefly, and pulled
herself onto the side of the pool, letting her legs
dangle in the water. "Sometimes I feel that way,"
she said. "I'm Carol Bukaty." She stuck out her
hand, very businesslike.

"Pat Fallon."

She wore a grey tank suit; she was slender and
small-breasted, tall, with a pointed chin and brown
eyes. Fallon later discovered that she was an excel-
lent dancer, that she purchased women's clothing
for one of the major Chicago department stores,
that she traveled a great deal, wrote lousy poetry,
disliked cooking, liked children, and liked him. At
first he was merely interested in her sexually,
though the first few times they slept together it was
not very good at all. Gradually the sex got better,
and in the meantime Fallon fell in love.

She would meet him at the athletic club after
work; they would play racquet ball in the late
afternoon, go out to dinner and take in a movie,
then spend the night at his or her apartment. He
met her alcoholic father, a retired policeman who
told endless stories about ward politics and the
Daley machine, and Carol spent a Christmas with
him at his parents'. After they moved in together,
they settled into a comfortable routine. He felt

secure in her affection for him. He did not want her, after a while, as much as he had that first day, those first months, but he still needed her. It still mattered to him what she was doing and what she thought of him. Sometimes it mattered to him too much, he thought. Sometimes he wanted to be without her at all, not because he had anything he could only do without her, but only because he wanted to *be* without her.

He would watch her getting dressed in the morning and wonder what creature she might be, and what that creature was doing in the same room with him. He would lie beside her as she slept, stroking the short brown hair at her temple with his fingertips, and be overwhelmed with the desire to possess her, to hold her head between his hands and know everything that she was; he would shake with the sudden frustration of its impossibility until it was all he could do to keep from striking her. Something was wrong with him, or with her. He had fantasies of how much she would miss him if he died, of what clothes she would wear to the funeral, of what stories she would tell her lovers in the future after he was gone.

If Carol felt any of the same things about him, she did not tell him. For Fallon's part, he did not try to explain what he felt in any but the most oblique ways. She should know how he felt, but of course she did not. So when things went badly, and they began to do so more and more, it was not possible for him to explain to her what was wrong, because he could not say it himself, and the pieces of his discontent were things that he was too embarrassed to admit. Yet he could not deny that sometimes he felt as if it was all over between them, that he felt nothing—and at others he would smile just to have her walk into the room.

Remarkable creature though the whale was, it was not so hard to kill one after all. It tired, just as a man would tire under the attack of a group of strangers. It slowed in the water, no longer able so effortlessly to drag them after it. They pulled close, and Stubb drove home the iron, jerked it back and forth, drew it out and drove it home again, fist over fist on the hilt, booted foot over the gunnel braced against the creature's flesh, sweating, searching for the whale's hidden life. At last he found it, and the whale shuddered and thrashed a last time, spouting pink mist, then dark blood, where once it spouted feathery white spray. Like a man, helpless in the end, it rolled over and died. Stubb was jolly, and the men were methodical; they tied their lines around the great tail and, as shadows grew long and the sun fell perpendicularly toward the horizon, drew the dead whale to the *Pequod*.

8

During the cutting up and boiling down of the whale that night, Fallon, perhaps in recognition of his return to normality as indicated by his return to the masthead, was given a real job: slicing the chunks of blubber that a couple of other sailors were hewing out of the great strips that were hauled over the side, into "bible leaves." Fallon got the hang of it pretty quickly, though he was not fast, and Staley, the British sailor who was cutting beside him, kept poking at him to do more. "I'm doing all the work, Fallon," he said, as if his ambition in life were to make sure that he did no more than his own share of the work.

Using a sharp blade like a long cleaver, Fallon would position the chunk of blubber, skin side down on the cutting table, and imitating Staley, cut the piece into slices like the pages of a book, with the skin as its spine. The blubber leaves flopped outward or stuck to each other, and the table became slick with grease. Fallon was at first careful about avoiding his hands, but the blubber would slide around the table as he tried to cut it if he didn't hold it still. Staley pushed him on, working with dexterity, though Fallon noted that the man's hands were scarred, with the top joint of the middle finger of his left hand missing.

His back and shoulders ached with fatigue, and the smoke from the try-works stung his eyes. When he tried to wipe the tears away, he only smeared his face with grease. But he did a creditable job, cursing all the time. The cursing helped, and the other men seemed to accept him more for it. When finally they were done, and the deck was clean the next day, they were issued a tot of grog and allowed to swim within the lee of the stationary ship. The men were more real to him than when he had sat and watched from the outcast's station of the tar bucket. He was able to speak to them more naturally than he had ever done. But he did not forget his predicament.

"Ye are too serious, Fallon," Staley told him, offering Fallon some of his grog. "I can see you brooding there, and look how it set you into a funk. Ye are better now, perhaps, but mind you stick to your work and ye may survive this voyage."

"I won't survive it. Neither will you—unless we can do something about Captain Ahab."

Bulkington, who had been watching them, came by. "What of Captain Ahab?"

Fallon saw a chance in this. "Does his seeking after this white whale seem right to you?"

"The whale took his leg," Staley said.

"Some say it unmanned him," the other said, lower. "That's two legs you'd not like to lose yourself, I'll daresay."

Fallon drew them aside, more earnest now. "We will lose more than our balls if we do nothing about this situation. The man is out of his mind. He will drag us all down with him, and this ship with all of us, if we can't convince Starbuck to do something. Believe me, I know."

Friendly Bulkington did not look so friendly. "You do talk strange, Fallon. We took an oath, and we signed the papers before we even sailed a cable from shore. A captain is a captain. You are talking mutiny."

He had to go carefully.

"No, wait. Listen to me. Why are we sent on this trip? Think of the—the stockholders, or whatever you call them. The owners. They sent us out to hunt whales."

"The white whale is a whale." Staley looked petulant.

"Yes, of course it's a whale. But there are hundreds of whales to be caught and killed. We don't need to hunt that one. Hasn't he set his sights on

just Moby Dick? What about that oath? That gold
piece on the mast? That says he's just out for
vengeance. There was nothing about vengeance in
the papers we signed. What do you think the
owners would say if they knew about what he
plans? Do you think they would approve of this
wild goose chase?"

Staley was lost. "Goose chase?"

Bulkington was interested. "Go on."

Fallon had his foot in the door; he marshaled the
arguments he had rehearsed over and over again.
"There's no more oil in Moby Dick than in another
whale . . ."

"They say he's monstrous big," Staley inter-
jected.

Fallon looked pained. "Not so big as any two
whales, then. Ahab is not after any oil you can boil
out of the whale's flesh. If the owners knew what
he intended, the way I do, if they knew how sick he
was the week before he came out of that hole of a
cabin he lives in, if they saw that light in his eye and
the charts he keeps in his cabinet . . ."

"Charts? What charts? Have you been in his
cabin?"

"No, not exactly," Fallon said. "Look, I know
some things, but that's just because I keep my eyes
open and I have some sources."

"Fallon, where do you hail from? I swear that I
cannot half the time make out what you are saying.
Sources? What do you mean by that?"

"Oh, Jesus!" He had hoped for better from
Bulkington.

Staley darkened. "Don't blaspheme, man! I'll not
take the word of a blasphemer."

Fallon saw another opening. "You're right! I'm
sorry. But look, didn't the old man himself blas-

pheme more seriously than I ever could the night of that oath? If you are a God-fearing man, Staley, you'll know that that is true. Would you give your obedience to such a man? Moby Dick is just another of God's creatures, a dumb animal. Is it right to seek vengeance on an animal? Do you want to be responsible for that? God would not approve."

Staley looked troubled, but stubborn. "Do not tell me what the Almighty approves. That is not for the likes of you to know. And Ahab is the captain." With that he walked to the opposite side of the deck and stood there watching them as if he wanted to separate himself as much as possible from the conversation, yet still know what was going on.

Fallon was exasperated and tired.

"Why don't you go with Staley, Bulkington? You don't have to stick around with me, you know. I'm not going to do your reputation any good."

Bulkington eyed him steadily. "You are a strange one, Fallon. I did not think anything of you when I first saw you on the *Pequod*. But you may be talking some sense."

"Staley doesn't think so."

Bulkington took a pull on his grog. "Why did you try to persuade Staley of Ahab's madness? You should have known that you couldn't convince such a man that the sky is blue, if it were written in the articles he signed that it was green. Starbuck perhaps, or me. Not Staley. Don't you listen to the man you are talking to?"

Fallon looked at Bulkington; the tall sailor looked calmly back at him, patient, waiting.

"Okay, you're right," Fallon said. "I have the feeling I would not have a hard time convincing you, anyway. You know Ahab's insane, don't you?"

"It's not for me to say. Ahab has better reasons than those you give to him." He drew a deep breath, looked up at the sky, down at the men who swam in the shadow of the ship. He smiled. "They should be more wary of sharks," he said.

"The world does look a garden today, Fallon. But it may be that the old man's eyes are better than ours."

"You know he's mad, and you won't do anything?"

"The matter will not bear too deep a looking into." Bulkington was silent for a moment. "You know the story about the man born with a silver screw in his navel? How it tasked him, until one day he unscrewed it to divine its purpose?"

Fallon had heard the joke in grade school on the South Side. "His ass fell off."

"You and Ahab are too much like that man."

They both laughed. "I don't have to unscrew my navel," Fallon said. "We're all going to lose our asses anyway."

They laughed again. Bulkington put his arm around his shoulders, and they toasted Moby Dick.

9

There came a morning when, on pumping out the bilge, someone noticed that considerable whale oil was coming up with the water. Starbuck was summoned and, after descending into the hold himself, emerged and went aft and below to speak with Ahab. Fallon asked one of the others what was going on.

"The casks are leaking. We're going to have to lay up and break them out. If we don't, we stand to lose a lot of oil."

Some time later Starbuck reappeared. His face was red to the point of apoplexy, and he paced around the quarter-deck with his hands knotted behind his back. They waited for him to tell them what to do; he stared at the crewmen, stopped, and told them to be about their business. "Keep pumping," he told the others. "Maintain the lookout." He then spoke briefly to the helmsman leaning on the whalebone tiller, and retreated to the corner of the quarter-deck to watch the wake of the ship. After a while Ahab himself staggered up onto the deck, found Starbuck, and spoke to him. He then turned to the men on deck.

"Furl the t'gallantsails," he called, "and close reef the topsails, fore and aft; back the main-yard; up Burtons, and break out in the main hold."

Fallon joined the others around the hold. Once the work had commenced, he concentrated on lifting, hauling, and not straining his back. The Manxman told them that he had been outside Ahab's cabin during the conference and that Ahab had threatened to shoot Starbuck dead on the spot when the mate demanded they stop chasing the whale to break out the hold. Fallon thought about the anger in Starbuck's face when he'd come up again. It struck him that the Starbuck of Melville's book was pretty ineffectual; he had to be to let that madman go on with the chase. But this Starbuck— whether like the one in the book or not—did not like the way things were going. There was no reason why Fallon had to sit around and wait for things to happen. It was worth a shot.

But not that afternoon.

Racism assured that the hardest work in the dank hold was done by the colored men—Dagoo, Tashtego, and Queequeg. They did not complain. Up to their knees in the bilge, clambering awkwardly over and about the barrels of oil in the murderous heat and unbreathable air of the hold, they did their jobs.

It was evening before the three harpooners were told they could halt for the day and they emerged, sweaty, covered with slime, and bruised. Fallon collapsed against the side of the try-works; others sat beside him. Tall Queequeg was taken by a coughing fit, then went below to his hammock. Fallon gathered his strength, felt the sweat drying stickily on his arms and neck. There were few clouds, and the moon was waxing full. He saw Starbuck then, standing at the rear of the quarterdeck, face toward the mast. Was he looking at the doubloon?

Fallon got shakily to his feet; his legs were rubbery. The first mate did not notice him until he was close. He looked up.

"Yes?"

"Mr. Starbuck, I need to speak to you."

Starbuck looked at him as if he saw him for the first time. Fallon tried to look self-confident, serious. He'd gotten that one down well at DCB.

"Yes?"

Fallon turned so that he was facing inward toward the deck and Starbuck had his back to it to face him. He could see what was happening away from them and would know if anyone came near.

"I could not help but see that you were angry this morning after speaking to Captain Ahab."

Starbuck looked puzzled.

"I assume that you must have told Ahab about the leaking oil, and he didn't want to stop his hunt of the whale long enough to break out the hold. Am I right?"

The mate watched him guardedly. "What passed between Captain Ahab and me was none of your affair, or of the crew's. Is that what you've come to trouble me with?"

"It is a matter that concerns me," Fallon said. "It concerns the rest of the crew, and it ought to concern you. We are being bound by his orders, and what kind of orders is he giving? I know what you've been thinking; I know that this personal vengeance he seeks frightens and repulses you. I *know* what you're thinking. I could see what was in your mind when you stood at this rail this afternoon. He is not going to stop until he kills us all."

Starbuck seemed to draw back within himself. Fallon saw how beaten the man's eyes were; he did not think the mate was a drinker, but he looked like someone who had just surfaced after a long weekend. He could almost see the clockwork turning within Starbuck, a beat too slow, with the belligerence of the drunk being told the truth about himself that he did not want to admit. Fallon's last fight with Stein Jr at the brokerage had started that way.

"Get back to your work," Starbuck said. He started to turn away.

Fallon put his hand on his shoulder. "You have to—"

Starbuck whirled with surprising violence and pushed Fallon away so that he nearly stumbled and fell. The man at the tiller was watching them.

"To work! You do not know what I am thinking! I'll have you flogged if you say anything more! A man with a three-hundreth lay has nothing to tell me. Go on, now."

Fallon was hot. "God damn you. You stupid—"

"Enough!" Starbuck slapped him with the back of his hand, the way Stein had tried to slap Fallon. Stein had missed. It appeared that Mr. Starbuck was more effectual than Stein Jr. Fallon felt his bruised cheek. The thing that hurt the most was the way he must have looked, like a hangdog insubordinate who had been shown his place. As Fallon stumbled away, Starbuck said, in a steadier voice, "Tend to your own conscience, man. Let me tend to mine."

10

Lightning flashed again.

"I now know that thy right worship is defiance. To neither love nor reverence wilt thou be kind; and even for hate thou canst but kill, and all are killed!"

Ahab had sailed them into the heart of a typhoon. The sails were in tatters, and the men ran across the deck shouting against the wind and trying to lash the boats down tighter before they were washed away or smashed. Stubb had gotten his left hand caught between one of the boats and the rail; he now held it with his right and grimaced. The mastheads were touched with St. Elmo's fire. Ahab stood with the lightning rod in his right hand and his right foot planted on the neck of Fedallah, declaiming at the lightning. Fallon held tightly to a shroud to keep from being thrown off his feet. The scene was ludicrous; it was horrible.

"No fearless fool now fronts thee!" Ahab shouted at the storm. "I own thy speechless, placeless power; but to the last gasp of my earthquake life will dispute its unconditional, unintegral mastery in me! In the midst of the personified impersonal, a personality stands here!"

Terrific, Fallon thought. Psychobabble. Melville writes in a storm so Ahab can have a backdrop

against which to define himself. They must not
have gone in for realism much in Melville's day. He
turned and tried to lash the rear quarter boat
tighter; its stern had already been smashed in by a
wave that had just about swept three men, includ-
ing Fallon, overboard. Lightning flashed, followed
a split-second later by the rolling thunder. Fallon
recalled that five-seconds' count meant the lightning was a mile away; by that measure the last bolt
must have hit them in the ass. Most of the crew
were staring open-mouthed at Ahab and the glowing, eerie flames that touched the masts. The light
had the bluish tinge of mercury vapor lamps in a
parking lot. It sucked the color out of things; the
faces of the frightened men were the sickly hue of
fish bellies.

"Thou canst blind, but I can then grope. Thou
canst consume, but I can then be ashes!" You bet.
"Take the homage of these poor eyes, and shutter-
hands. I would not take it . . ." Ahab ranted on.
Fallon hardly gave a damn anymore. The book was
too much. Ahab talked to the storm and the God
behind it; the storm answered him back, lightning
flash for curse. It was dramatic, stagy; it was real:
Melville's universe was created so that such dia-
logues could take place; the howling gale and the
tons of water, the crashing waves, flapping canvas,
the sweating, frightened men, the blood and
seawater—all were created to have a particular
effect, to be sure, but it was the real universe, and it
would work that way because that was the way it
was set up to work by a frustrated, mystified man
chasing his own obsessions, creating the world as a
warped mirror of his distorted vision.

"There is some unsuffusing thing beyond thee,

thou clear spirit, to whom all thy eternity is but time, all thy creativeness mechanical . . .''

There is an ex-sailor on a farm in Massachusetts trying to make ends meet while his puzzled wife tries to explain him to the relatives.

"The boat! The boat!" cried Starbuck. "Look at thy boat, old man!"

Fallon looked, and backed away. A couple of feet from him the harpoon that was lashed into the bow was tipped with the same fire that illuminated the masts. Silently within the howling storm, from its barbed end twin streamers of electricity writhed. Fallon backed away to the rail, heart beating quickly, and clutched the slick whalebone.

Ahab staggered toward the boat; Starbuck grabbed his arm. "God! God is against thee, old man! Forbear! It's an ill voyage! Ill begun, ill continued; let me square the yards while we may, old man, and make a fair wind of it homewards, to go on a better voyage than this."

Yes, yes, at last Starbuck had said it! Fallon grabbed one of the braces; he saw others of the crew move to the rigging as if to follow Starbuck's order before it was given. They cried, some of them in relief, others in fear, others as if ready at last to mutiny. Yes!

Ahab threw down the last links of the lightning rod. He grabbed the harpoon from the boat and waved it like a torch about his head; he lurched toward Fallon.

"You!" he shouted, staggering to maintain his balance on the tossing deck, hoisting the flaming harpoon to his shoulder as if he meant to impale Fallon on the spot. "But cast loose that rope's end and you will be transfixed—by this clear spirit!"

The electricity at the barb hummed inches before him; Fallon could feel his skin prickling and smelled ozone. He felt the rail at the small of his back, cold. The other sailors fell away from the ropes; Starbuck looked momentarily sick. Fallon let go of the brace.

Ahab grinned at him. He turned and held the glowing steel before him with both hands like a priest holding a candle at mass on a feast day.

"All your oaths to hunt the white whale are as binding as mine; and heart, soul, and body, lung and life, old Ahab is bound. And that you may know to what tune this heart beats; look ye here! Thus I blow out the last fear!"

He blew out the flame.

They ran out the night without letting the anchors over the side, heading due into the gale instead of riding with the wind at their backs, with tarpaulins and deck truck blown or washed overboard, with the lightning rod shipped instead of trailing in the sea as it ought to, with the man at the tiller beaten raw about the ribs trying to keep the ship straight, with the compass spinning round like a top, with the torn remains of the sails not cut away until long after midnight.

By morning the storm had much abated, the wind had come around, and they ran before it in heavy seas. Fallon and most of the other common sailors, exhausted, were allowed to sleep.

11

The argument with Starbuck and his attempts to rouse others to defy Ahab had made Fallon something of a pariah. He was now as isolated as he had been when he'd first come to himself aboard the *Pequod*. Only Bulkington did not treat him with contempt or fear, but Bulkington would do nothing about the situation. He would rather talk, and they often discussed what a sane man would do in their situation, given the conflicting demands of reason and duty. Fallon's ability to remain detached always failed him somewhere in the middle of these talks.

So Fallon came to look upon his stints at the masthead as escape of a sort. It was there that he had first realized that he could rise above the deck of the *Pequod*, both literally and figuratively, for some moments; it was there that he had first asserted his will after days of stunned debility. He would not sing out for the white whale, if it should be his fortune to sight it, but he did sing out more than once for lesser whales. The leap of his heart at the sight of them was not feigned.

They were sailing the calm Pacific east and south of Japan. They had met the *Rachel*, and a thrill had run through the crew at the news that she had encountered Moby Dick and had failed to get him, losing several boats, and the captain's son, in the process. Fallon's memory was jogged. The *Rachel* would pick up Ishmael at the end of the book, when all the others were dead.

They met the *Delight*, on which a funeral was in progress. From the mainmast lookout, Fallon heard the shouted talk between Ahab and her captain about another failed attempt at the white whale. He watched as the dead man, sewn up in his hammock, was dropped into the sea.

It was a clear, steel-blue day. The sea rolled in long, quiet swells; the *Pequod* moved briskly ahead before a fair breeze, until the *Delight* was lost in the distance astern. The air was fresh and clear out to the rim of the world, where it seemed to merge with the darker sea. It was as fair a day as they had seen since Fallon had first stood a watch at the masthead.

Up above the ship, almost out of the world of men entirely, rolling at the tip of the mast in rhythm to the rolling of the sea swells, which moved in time with his own easy breathing, Fallon lost his fear. He seemed to lose even himself. Who was he? Patrick Fallon, analyst for a commodities firm. Perhaps that had been some delusion; perhaps that world had been created somewhere inside of him, pressed upon him in a vision. He was a sailor on the *Pequod*. He thought that this was part of some book, but he had not been a reader for many years.

Memories of his other life persisted. He remembered the first time he had ever made love to a woman—to Sally Torrance, in the living room of her parents' house while they were away skiing in Minnesota. He remembered cutting his palm playing baseball when the bat had shattered in his hand. The scar in the middle of his hand could not be denied.

Who denied it? He watched an albatross swoop down from above him to skim a few feet above the water, trying to snag some high-leaping fish. It turned away, unsuccessful, beating its wings slowly as it climbed the air. There was rhythm to its unconscious dance. Fallon had never seen anything more beautiful. He hung his arms over the hoop that surrounded him, felt the hot sun beating on his back, the band of metal supporting him.

This was the real world; he accepted it. He accepted the memories that contradicted it. I look, you look, he looks. Could his mind and heart hold two contradictory things? What would happen to him then? He accepted the albatross, the fish, the sharks he could see below the water's surface from his high vantage point. He accepted the grace of the sea, its embrace on this gentlest of days, and he accepted the storm that had tried to kill them only days before. The *Delight*, reason told him—let reason be; he could strain reason no further than he had—the *Delight* might perhaps have been a ship from a story he had read, but he had no doubt that the man who had been dropped to his watery grave as Fallon watched had been a real man.

The blue of sky and sea, the sound of the flag snapping above him, the taste of the salt air, the motion of the sea and earth itself as they swung Fallon at the tip of the mast, the memories and speculations, the feel of warm sun and warm iron—all the sensual world flowed together for Fallon then. He could not say what he felt. Joy that he could hardly contain swelled in his chest. He was at one with all his perceptions, with all he knew and remembered, with Carol, wherever or whatever she might be, with Bulkington and Dagoo and Starbuck and Stein Jr. and the Big House and Queequeg and the CBT and Ahab. Ahab.

Why had Fallon struggled so long against it? He was alive. What thing had driven him to fight so hard? What had happened to him was absurd, but what thing was not absurd? What thing had made him change from the student to the dropout to the analyst to the sailor? Who might Patrick Fallon be? He stretched out his right arm and turned his hand in the sun.

"Is it I, or God, or who, that lifts this arm?" Fallon heard the words quite distinctly, as if they were spoken only for him, as if they were not spoken at all but were only thoughts. God perhaps did lift Fallon's arm, and if that were so, then who was Fallon to question the wisdom or purpose of the motion? It was his only to move.

A disturbance in the blue of the day.

Why should he not have a choice? Why should that God give him the feeling of freedom if in fact He was directing Fallon's every breath? Did the Fates weave this trance-like calm blue day to lead Fallon to these particular conclusions, so that not even his thoughts in the end were his own, but only the promptings of some force beyond him? And what force could that be if not the force that created this world, and who created this world but Herman Melville, a man who had been dead for a very long time, a man who had no possible connection with Fallon? And what could be the reason for the motion? If this was the real world, then why had Fallon been given the life he had lived before, tangled himself in, felt trapped within, only to be snatched away and clumsily inserted into a different fantasy? What purpose did it serve? Whose satisfaction was being sought?

The moment of wholeness died; the world dissolved into its disparate elements. The sea rolled on. The ship fought it. The wind was opposed by straining canvas. The albatross dove once again, and skimming over the surface so fast it was a white blur, snatched a gleam of silver—a flying fish—from midflight. It settled to the ocean's surface, tearing at its prey.

The day was not so bright as it had been. Fallon tried to accept it still. He did not know if there was a malign force behind the motion of the earth in its long journey, or a beneficent one whose purpose was merely veiled to men such as himself—or no force at all. Such knowledge would not be his. He was a sailor on the *Pequod*.

Upon descending, Fallon heard from Bulkington that Starbuck and Ahab had had a conversation about turning back to Nantucket, that the mate had seemed almost to persuade the captain to give up the hunt, but that he had failed.

Fallon knew then that they must be coming to the end of the story. It would not be long before they spotted the white whale, and three days after that the *Pequod* would go down with all hands not previously killed in the encounter with the whale —save one. But Fallon had given up the idea that he might be that one. He did not, despite his problems, qualify as an Ishmael. That would be overstating his importance, he thought.

12

He woke suddenly to the imperative buzzing of his alarm clock. His heart beat very fast. He tried to slow it by breathing deeply. Carol stirred beside him, then slept again.

He felt disoriented. He walked into the bathroom, staring, as if he had never seen it before. He slid open the mirrored door of the medicine chest and looked inside at the almost-empty tube of toothpaste, the old safety razor, the pack of double-edged blades, the darvon and tetracycline capsules, the foundation make-up. When he slid the door shut again, his tanned face looked back at him.

He was slow getting started that morning; when Carol got up, he was still drinking his coffee, with the radio playing an old Doors song in the background. Carol leaned over him, kissed the top of his head. It appeared that she loved him.

"You'd better get going," she said. "You'll be late."

He hadn't worried about being late, and it hit him for the first time what he had to do. He had to get to the Board of Trade. He'd have to talk to Stein Jr, and there would be a sheaf of notes on his desk asking him to return calls to various clients who would have rung him up while he was gone. He pulled on the jacket of his pinstriped suit, brushed back his hair, and left.

Waiting for the train, he realized that he hadn't gone anywhere to return from.

He had missed his normal train and arrived late. The streets were nowhere near as crowded as they would have been an hour earlier. He walked north on LaSalle Avenue between the staid, dark old buildings. The sky that showed between them was bright, and already the temperature was rising; it would be a hot one. He wished it were the weekend. Was it Thursday? It couldn't still be Wednesday. He was embarrassed to realize he wasn't sure what day it was.

He saw a very pretty girl in the lobby of the Board of Trade as he entered through the revolving doors. She was much prettier than Carol, and had that unself-conscious way of walking. But she was around the corner before he had taken more than a few steps inside. He ran into Joe Wendelstadt in the elevator, and Joe began to tell him a story about Raoul Lark from Brazil who worked for Cacex in Chicago, and how Lark had tried to pick up some feminist the other night. And succeeded. Those Brazilians.

Fallon got off before Joe could reach the climax. In his office Molly, the receptionist, said Stein wanted to see him. Stein smelled of cigarettes, and Fallon suddenly became self-conscious. He had not brushed his own teeth. When did he ever forget that? Stein had an incipient zit on the end of his nose. He didn't really have anything to talk to Fallon about; he was just wasting time as usual.

Tigue was sick or on vacation.

Fallon worked through the morning on various customer accounts. He had trouble remembering

where the market had closed the day before. He
had always had a trick memory for such figures,
and it had given him the ability to impress a lot of
people who knew just as much about the markets
as he did. He spent what was left of the morning on
the phone to his clients, with a quick trip down to
the trading floor to talk to Parsons in the soybean
pit.

Carol called and asked him if he could join her
for lunch. He remembered he had a date with Kim,
a woman from the CME he had met just a week
before. He made his excuses to Carol and took off
for the Merc.

Walking briskly west on Jackson, coming up on
the bridge across the river, he realized he had been
rushing around all day and yet could hardly remember what he'd done since he had woken up.
He still couldn't remember whether it was Wednesday or Thursday.

As he crossed the bridge with the crowds of
lunch-hour office workers, the noontime sun
glared brightly for a second from the oily water of
the river. Fallon's eyes did not immediately recover. He stopped walking and somebody bumped
into him.

"Excuse me," he said unconsciously.

There was a moment of silence, then the noise of
the city resumed, and he could see again. He stood
at the side of the bridge and looked down at the
water. The oil on the surface made rainbow-
colored black swirls. Fallon shook his head and
went on.

Kim stood him up at the restaurant. She did not
arrive to meet him, and he waited a long time by
the cashier. Finally he made the woman seat him at
a table for two. He looked at his watch but had

some trouble reading the time. Was he due back at the office?

Just then someone sat down opposite him. It was an old man in a dark suit who had obviously undergone some great ordeal. His face held a look of great pain or sorrow—with hate burning just beneath it. Though his hair was black (and quite unforgivably unkempt for midtown Chicago, as was his rough suit), a shock of white fell across his forehead, and a scar ran from the roots of that white hair straight down the man's face, leaping the brow and eye to continue across the left cheek, sinewing down the jaw and neck to disappear beneath his shirt collar.

He looked strangely familiar.

"It won't work," the man said. "You cannot get away. You have signed the articles, like the rest, and are in for a three-hundreth lay."

"Three-hundreth lay?" Fallon was bewildered.

"A three-hundreth part of the general catastrophe is yours. Don't thank me. It isn't necessary." The old man looked even more sorrowful and more wild, if it were possible to combine those seemingly incompatible emotions.

"To tell you the truth," he said, "I wouldn't hold you to the contract if it were strictly up to me." He shrugged his shoulders and opened his palms before him. "But it isn't."

Fallon's heart was beating fast again. "I don't remember any contract. You're not one of my clients. I don't trade for you. I've been in this business for a long time, mister, and I know better than to sign . . ."

The wildness swelled in the man. There was something burning in him, and he looked about to scream, or cry.

"*I* have been in the business longer than *you*!" He swung his leg out from beneath the table and rapped it loudly with his knuckle. Fallon saw that the leg was of white bone. "And I can tell *you* that you signed the contract when you signed aboard this ship—there's no other way to get aboard—and you must serve until you strike land again or it sinks beneath you!"

The diners in the restaurant dined on, oblivious. Fallon looked toward the plate glass at the front of the room and saw the water rising rapidly up it, sea-green and turbid, as the restaurant and the city fell to the bottom of the sea.

13

Once again he was jerked awake, this time by the din of someone beating the deck of the forecastle above them with a club. The other sleepers were as startled as Fallon. He rolled out of the hammock with the mists of his dream still clinging to him, pulled on his shirt and scrambled up to the deck.

Ahab was stalking the quarter-deck in a frenzy of impatience. "Man the mastheads!" he shouted.

The men who had risen with Fallon did just that, some of them only half-dressed. Fallon was one of the first up and gained one of the hoops at the main masthead. Three others stood on the mainyard below him. Fallon scanned the horizon and saw off to starboard and far ahead of them the jet of mist that indicated a whale. As it rose and fell in its course through the rolling seas, Fallon saw that it was white.

"What do you see?" Ahab called from far below. Had he noticed Fallon's gaze fixed on the spot in front of them?

"Nothing! Nothing, sir!" Fallon called. Ahab and the men on deck looked helpless so far below him. Fallon did not know if his lying would work, but there was the chance that the other men in the rigging, not being as high as he, would not be able to make out Moby Dick from their lower vantage points. He turned away from the whale and made a good show of scanning the empty horizon.

"Top gallant sails!—stunsails! Alow and aloft, and on both sides!" Ahab ordered. The men fixed a line from the mainmast to the deck, looped its lower end around Ahab's rigid leg. Ahab wound the rope around his shoulders and arm, and they hoisted him aloft, twisting with the pressure on the hemp, toward the masthead. He twirled slowly as they raised him up, and his line of sight was obscured by the rigging and sails he had to peer through.

Before they had lifted him two-thirds of the way up, he began to shout.

"There she blows!—there she blows! A hump like a snowhill! It is Moby Dick!"

Fallon knew enough to begin shouting and pointing immediately, and the men at the other two masts did the same. Within a minute everyone who had remained on the deck was in the rigging trying to catch a glimpse of the creature they had sought, half of them doubting his existence, for so many months.

Fallon looked down toward the helmsman, who stood on his toes, the whalebone tiller under his arm, arching his neck trying to see the whale.

The others in the rigging were now arguing about who had spotted Moby Dick first, with Ahab the eventual victor. It was his fate, he said, to be the one to first spot the whale. Fallon couldn't argue with that.

Ahab was lowered to the deck, giving orders all the way, and three boats were swung outboard in preparation for the chase. Starbuck was ordered to stay behind and keep the ship.

As they chased the whale, the sea became calmer, so the rowing became easier—though just as back-breaking—and they knifed through the water, here as placid as a farm pond, faster than ever. Accompanying the sound of their own wake, Fallon heard the wake of the whale they must be approaching. He strained arms, back, and legs, pulling harder in time to Stubb's cajoling chant, and the rushing grew. He snatched a glance over his shoulder, turned to the rowing, then looked again.

The white whale glided through the sea smoothly, giving the impression of immeasurable strength. The wake he left was as steady as that of a schooner; the bow waves created by the progress of his broad, blank brow through the water fanned away in precise lines whose angle with respect to the massive body did not change. The three whaleboats rocked gently as they broke closer through these successive waves; the foam of Moby Dick's wake was abreast of them now, and Fallon saw how quickly it subsided into itself, giving the sea back its calm face, innocent of knowledge of the creature that had passed. Attendant white birds circled above their heads, now and then falling to or rising from the surface in busy flutterings of wings and awkward beaks. One of them had landed on the broken shaft of a harpoon that protruded from the snow-white whale's humped back; it bobbed up and down with the slight rocking of the whale in its long, muscular surging through the sea. Oblivious. Strangely quiet. Fallon felt as if they had entered a magic circle.

He knew Ahab's boat, manned by the absurd Filipinos, was ahead of them and no doubt preparing to strike first. Fallon closed his eyes, pulled on his oar, and wished for it not to happen. For it to stop now, or just continue without any change. He felt as if he could row a very long time; he was no longer tired or afraid. He just wanted to keep rowing, feeling the rhythm of the work, hearing the low and insistent voice of Stubb telling them to break their backs. Fallon wanted to listen to the rushing white sound of the whale's wake in the water, to know that they were perhaps keeping pace with it, to know that, if he should tire, he could look for a second over his shoulder and find Moby Dick there still. Let the monomaniac stand in the bow of his boat—if he was meant to stand there, if it was an unavoidable necessity—let him stand there with the raised lance and concentrate his hate into one purified moment of will. Let him send that will into the tip of that lance so that it might physically glow with the frustrated obtuseness of it. Let him stand there until he froze from the suspended desire, and let the whale swim on.

Fallon heard a sudden increase in the rushing of the water, several inarticulate cries. He stopped pulling, as did the others, and turned to look in time to see the whale lift itself out of the water, exposing flanks and flukes the bluish white of cemetery marble, and flip its huge tail upward to dive perpendicularly into the sea. Spray drenched them, and sound returned with the crash of the waves coming together to fill the vacuum left by the departure of the creature that had seconds before given weight and direction, place, to the placeless expanse of level waters. The birds circled above the subsiding foam.

They lifted their oars. They waited.

"An hour," Ahab said.

They waited. It was another beautiful day. The sky was hard and blue as the floor of the swimming pool where he had met Carol. Fallon wondered again if she missed him, if he had indeed disappeared from that other life when he had taken up residence in this one—but he thrust those thoughts away. They were meaningless. There was no time in that world after his leaving it; that world did not exist, or if it existed, the order of its existence was not of the order of the existence of the rough wood he sat on, the raw flesh of his hands and the air he breathed. Time was the time between the breaths he drew. Time was the duration of the dream he had had about being back in Chicago, and he could not say how long that had been, even if it had begun or ended. He might be dreaming still. The word "dream" was meaningless, and "awake." And "real," and "insane," and "known," and all those other interesting words he had once known. Time was waiting for Moby Dick to surface again.

The breeze freshened. The sea began to swell.

"The birds!—the birds!" Tashtego shouted, so close behind Fallon's ear that he winced. The Indian half-stood, rocking the whaleboat as he pointed to the sea birds, which had risen and were flying toward Ahab's boat twenty yards away.

"The whale will breach there," Stubb said.

Ahab was up immediately. Peering into the water, he leaned on the steering oar and reversed the orientation of his boat. He then exchanged places with Fedallah, the other men reaching up to help him through the rocking boat. He picked up the harpoon, and the oarsmen stood ready to row.

Fallon looked down into the sea, trying to make out what Ahab saw. Nothing, until a sudden explosion of white as the whale, rocketing upward, turned over as it finally hit the surface. In a moment Ahab's boat was in the whale's jaws, Ahab in the bows almost between them. Stubb was shouting and gesturing, and Fallon's fellows fell to the oars in a disorganized rush. The Filipinos in the lead boat crowded into the stern while Ahab, like a man trying to open a recalcitrant garage door, tugged and shoved at Moby Dick's jaw, trying insanely to dislodge the whale's grip. Within seconds filled with crashing water, cries and confusion, Moby Dick had bitten the boat in two, and Ahab had belly-flopped over the side like a swimming-class novice.

Moby Dick then began to swim tight circles around the smashed boat and its crew. Ahab struggled to keep his head above water. Neither Stubb nor Flask could bring his boat close enough to pick him up. The *Pequod* was drawing nearer, and finally Ahab was able to shout loudly enough to be heard, "Sail on the whale—drive him off!"

It worked. The *Pequod* picked up the remnants of the whaleboat while Fallon and the others dragged its crew and Ahab into their own boat.

The old man collapsed in the bottom of the boat, gasping for breath, broken and exhausted. He moaned and shook. Fallon was sure he was finished whale chasing, that Stubb and the others would see the man was used up, that Starbuck would take over and sail them home. But in a minute or two Ahab was leaning on his elbow asking after his boat's crew, and a few minutes after that they had resumed the chase with double oarsmen in Stubb's boat.

Moby Dick drew steadily away as exhaustion wore them down. Fallon did not feel he could row any more after all. The *Pequod* picked them up and they gave chase in vain under all sail until dark.

14

On the second day's chase all three boats were smashed in. Many suffered sprains and contusions, and one was bitten by a shark. Ahab's whale-bone leg was shattered, with a splinter driven into his own flesh. Fedallah, who had been the captain's second shadow, was tangled in the line Ahab had shot into the white whale, dragged out of the boat, and drowned. Moby Dick escaped.

15

It came down to what Fallon had known it would come down to eventually.

In the middle of that night he went to talk to Ahab, who slept in one of the hatchways as he had the night before. The carpenter was making him another leg, wooden this time, and Ahab was curled sullenly in the dark lee of the after scuttle. Fallon did not know whether he was waiting or asleep.

He started down the stairs, hesitated on the second step. Ahab lifted his head. "What do you need?" he asked.

Fallon wondered what he wanted to say. He looked at the man huddled in the darkness and tried to imagine what moved him, tried to see him as a man instead of a thing. Was it possible he was only a man, or had Fallon himself become stylized and distorted by living in the book of Melville's imagination?

"You said—talking to Starbuck today—you said that everything that happens is fixed, decreed. You said it was rehearsed a billion years before any of it took place. Is it true?"

Ahab straightened and leaned toward Fallon, bringing his face into the dim light thrown by the lamps on deck. He looked at him for a moment in silence.

"I don't know. So it seemed as the words left my lips. The Parsee is dead before me, as he fortold. I don't know."

"That is why you're hunting the whale."

"That is why I'm hunting the whale."

"How can this hunt, how can killing an animal tell you anything? How can it justify your life? What satisfaction can it give you in the end, even if you boil it all down to oil, even if you cut Moby Dick into bible-leaves and eat him? I don't understand it."

The captain looked at him earnestly. He seemed to be listening, and leaping ahead of the questions. It was very dark in the scuttle, and they could hardly see each other. Fallon kept his hands folded tightly behind him. The blade of the cleaver he had shoved into his belt lay cool against the skin at the small of his back; it was the same knife he used to butcher the whale.

"If it is immutably fixed, then it does not matter what I do. The purpose and meaning are out of my hands, and thine. We have only to take our parts, to be the thing that it is written for us to be. Better to live that role given us than to struggle against it or play the coward, when the actions must be the same nonetheless. Some say I am mad to chase the whale. Perhaps I am mad. But if it is my destiny to seek him, to tear, to burn and kill those things that stand in my path—then the matter of my madness is not relevant, do you see?"

He was not speaking in character.

"If these things are not fixed, and it was not my destiny to have my leg taken by the whale, to have my hopes blasted in this chase, then how cruel a

world it is. No mercy, no power but its own
controls it; it blights our lives out of merest whim.
No, not whim, for there would then be no will
behind it, no builder of this Bedlam hospital, and
in the madhouse, when the keeper is gone, what is
to stop the inmates from doing as they please? In a
universe of cannibals, where all creatures have
preyed upon each other, carrying on an eternal
war since the world began, why should I not exert
my will in whatever direction I choose? Why
should I not bend others to my will?" The voice
was reasonable, and tired. "Have I answered your
question?"

Fallon felt the time drawing near. He felt light, as
if the next breeze might lift him from the deck and
carry him away. "I have an idea," he said. "My idea
is—and it is an idea I have had for some time now,
and despite everything that has happened, and
what you say, I can't give it up—my idea is that all
that is happening . . ." Fallon waved his hand at the
world, ". . . is a story. It is a book written by a man
named Herman Melville and told by a character
named Ishmael. You are the main character in the
book. All the things that have happened are events
in the book.

"My idea also is that I am not from the book, or
at least I wasn't originally. Originally I lived a
different life in another time and place, a life in the
real world and not in a book. It was not ordered
and plotted like a book, and. . . ."

Ahab interrupted in a quiet voice: "You call this
an ordered book? I see no order. If it were so
orderly, why would the whale task me so?"

Fallon knotted his fingers tighter behind him.
Ahab was going to make him do it. He felt the
threads of the situation weaving together to create

only that bloody alternative, of all the alternatives that might be. In the open market, the price for the future and price for the physical reality converged on delivery day.

"The order's not an easy thing to see, I'll admit," Fallon said. He laughed nervously.

Ahab laughed louder. "It certainly is not. And how do you know this other life you speak of was not a play? A different kind of play. How do you know your thoughts are your own? How do you know that this dark little scene was not prepared just for us, or perhaps for someone who is reading about us at this very moment and wondering about the point of the drama just as much as we wonder at the pointlessness of our lives?" Ahab's voice rose, gaining an edge of compulsion. "How do we know anything?" He grabbed his left wrist, pinched the flesh and shook it.

"How do we know what lies behind this matter? This flesh is a wall, the painting over the canvas, the mask drawn over the player's face, the snow fallen over the fertile field, or perhaps the scorched earth. I know there is something there; there must be something, but it cannot be touched because we are smothered in this flesh, this life. How do we know—"

"Stop it! Stop it!" Fallon shouted. "Please stop asking things! You should not be able to say things like that to me! Ahab does not talk to me!"

"Isn't this what I am supposed to say?"

Fallon shuddered.

"Isn't this scene in your book?"

He was dizzy, sick. "No! Of course not!"

"Then why does that disturb you? Doesn't this prove that we are not pieces of a larger dream, that this is a real world, that the blood that flows within

our veins is real blood, that the pain we feel has
meaning, that the things we do have consequence?
We break the mold of existence by existing. Isn't
that reassurance enough?" Ahab was shouting
now, and the men awake on deck trying to get the
boats in shape for the last day's chase and the
Pequod's ultimate destruction put aside their ham-
mers and rope and listened to his justification.

It was time. Fallon, shaking with anger and fear,
drew the knife from behind him and leapt at the
old man. In bringing up the blade for the attack he
hit it against the side of the narrow hatchway. His
grip loosened. Ahab threw up his hands, and
despite the difference in age and mobility between
them, managed to grab Fallon's wrist before he
could strike the killing blow. Instead, the deflected
cleaver struck the beam beside Ahab's head and
stuck there. As Fallon tried to free it, Ahab brought
his forearm up and smashed him beneath the jaw.
Fallon fell backward, striking his head with stun-
ning force against the opposite side of the scuttle.
He momentarily lost consciousness.

When he came to himself again, Ahab was sitting
before him with his strong hands on Fallon's
shoulders, supporting him, not allowing him to
move.

"Good, Fallon, good," he said. "You've done
well. But now, no more games, no more dramas,
no easy way out. Admit that this is not the tale you
think it is! Admit that you do not know what will
happen to you in the next second, let alone the next
day or year! Admit that we are both free and
unfree, alone and crowded in by circumstance in
this world that we indeed did not make, but indeed
have the power to affect! Put aside those notions
that there is another life somehow more real than

the life you live now, another air to breathe somehow more pure, another love or hate somehow
more vital than the love or hate you bear me. Put
aside your fantasy and admit that you are alive,
and thus may momentarily die. Do you hear me,
Fallon?"

Fallon heard, and saw, and felt and touched,
but he did not know. The *Pequod*, freighted with savages and isolatoes, sailed into the night, and the
great shroud of the sea rolled on as it rolled five
thousand years ago.

Coming soon in paperback from Tor Books:

Divine Endurance
by Gwyneth Jones

A very special science fiction novel concerning a cat named Divine Endurance, her young girl, and their lives in an inconceivably distant future.

Tor is pleased to offer this special preview excerpt from *Divine Endurance* for your reading pleasure.

My name is Divine Endurance. I am feminine. I am twenty-five small units high at the shoulder, and sixty-two small units long from nose to tail tip. I am independent and it is therefore the more flattering when I respond to affection. I am graceful, agile and especially good at killing things prettily. I live with the Empress and the Emperor. There are only three of us now. Once there were more of them: more Empresses and Emperors, and other names too, but things have been running down for a long time and gradually people fade away and one sees them no more. But I have never liked bustle, and I was perfectly happy until our troubles began. We have a pleasant life. We have our extensive palace, and our gardens where the light is always changing. We have outings to view the sunset and the dawn and the moon; we have lizards and flowers, warm rocks and cool shadows. There are certain restrictions: for instance, we are not supposed to go outside the gardens. But most of the time keeping the rules is simply common sense. I have explored the way to the glass basin, but the air down there smells horrible, and the light makes one's head ache. I have also been out towards the glass plateau, which is a shiny line on the sky to the west of our palace, but I found nothing of interest, only a few dirty places where some passing nomads had been camping. We are not to go near these people. If ever somebody wants one of us they will approach through the proper channels, and with some ceremony no doubt. Meanwhile, if the gypsies come too close to the palace (they don't often dare) we simply think discouraging thoughts and make ourselves scarce.

I should say that there is one rule that the Empress and the Emperor obey, which I ignore because it is just silly. When one of them grows past the point of being a child, they start talking what they call medicine. It is an effluent from the Controller. Once, when we all stayed inside, they used to line up and the Controller would give it to them in little cups out of a wall. But I think the wall or the cups faded away, and now they just drink it from their hands. It does them nothing but harm. The effects are slow but horrible. Their hair falls out, their muscles waste away, their skin grows flabby and their teeth crumble. Eventually some accident happens and the victim is too weak to recover, and that is the end. If they waited till they were properly grown up it would do them no harm— if they must have the stuff, but they won't. I do not remember ever being told to take this medicine. I do not know why they keep on doing it.

I think it was because of the medicine that I encouraged Em and Emp when they bagan to talk about a baby. They were both beginning to look quite sickly, and I do not think I would like to live entirely alone. They could not decide which kind of baby to have—they can never agree about anything—so they wanted one of each. I thought that two was excessive and would spoil our quiet times, but they went to the Controller anyway. There we had a shock: the Controller said we could only have one baby, because there was only one baby ability left. This was startling. It had seemed, I suppose, that things could go on running down forever and never completely stop. Could it be twins? asked Em. That's not allowed, said the Controller. We did not ask for the one baby to be started. We came away disappointed. But Em (I should have paid more attention) was thinking, privately and hard.

As I know, from my expeditions, nobody can actually prevent us if we want to disobey. When the Controller said "that's not allowed" rather than "not possible" I should have known what Em would do. Anyway, she did it. She went down into the Controller's entrails and made it do what it should not. It was wrong of her of course, but we have been left to our own devices for so long it is not at all fair to expect 'not allowed' to be enough, without any explanation.

The first I knew of Em's naughtiness at this point was that two hatches in the Controller began to go milky, and in a little while we could see the babies growing inside. This was a very strange sight, after so long. It was so interesting that Emp soon forgot to be shocked, and I to be displeased. We picked names. We made them up ourselves, we didn't see why not. Something simple and boyish for Emp's choice: Worthy to be Beloved. The girl's name was subtler: Chosen Among the Beautiful—implying 'chosen to be the best of the best', without quite saying so. We took sides and laid small bets on which was taking shape faster. We spent whole days just watching.

But Em had done wrong, and gradually it began to affect her. She stopped coming to see the babies. She hid herself away and brooded. Emp had a bad conscience too. He sat with his baby still, but now he was always sighing and sniffing. "Poor little mite," I heard him mutter. "We should never have started this. What a life . . . !" To make matters worse the weather was very unsettled. We do not usually have to suffer anything tiresome, like excessive wind or rain, but just now a lot of dust and sand got into the air and started blowing about; the sky was obscured and there were unpleasant smells. It was like being at the glass basin. Then one day there was an earth tremor. It was an unusual one because the disturbance seemed to start near at hand, rather than off somewhere in the distance. I was sitting with Em, in a distant quarter of the palace, trying to cheer her up. We were both a little shaken. A crowd of bats pelted squeaking from a dark passage beyond Em's corner, and three big lizards ran out of the wall. Em got up. "It's no good," she muttered, "I will have to stop it."

I ignored the lizards—I am very fond of Em—and followed her out of the room, trying to make her see that an earth tremor is harmless and she was being silly. She was stumbling on the uncertain ground on her poor wasted legs. I must admit I thought her mind was upset. Anyway I went with her, at her slow pace, to the Controller. There we found that one of the hatches had been torn open, and the boy baby was gone.

"It wasn't an earth tremor," said Em. "It was the Controller. We have frightened it."

She was very distressed. Not understanding, I assured her that the baby would have been nearly ready; it wouldn't be harmed. But she insisted that we start searching for Emp at once. We could not find him. We searched and searched for days, but he did not reappear. He had gone right away from the palace, which is not allowed. Now I realized what Em had somehow guessed all along: something serious had happened. It was difficult for us to follow him because Em moves so badly nowadays, but eventually we found his trail leading to the west. There, out in the wilderness, we found the dirty camp. It was already abandoned. They never stay anywhere long, but events had left enough of an impression for us to know beyond doubt what Emp had done. He had stolen our baby, taken it out of our world, and given it away to the gypsies.

There was nothing we could do, so we returned to the palace. Em was so angry she wouldn't talk to me. She tried to get the Controller to take her baby back—anything rather than let Emp have it, I suppose. The Controller was unresponsive. So the baby stayed behind the hatch, which was clear and filmy now, so the poor thing should have been taken out. And Em stayed inside the Controller, on guard. Meanwhile I discovered Emp, lurking in the north-east apartments. But he was unrepentant, so there seemed no hope of making up the quarrel. He even wanted me to get Em to give her baby away as well. Em, on the other hand, would not listen to any of my suggestions. When I said I would get Emp to swear solemnly to leave her baby alone she just stared at me scornfully. However, I persevered, trying to make peace and restore our former pleasant existence. When Em began to ask me how the Emperor was passing his time these days, I thought I was succeeding.

I know better now, and now there are only two of us. She came looking for me, when it was over and we both knew he was gone. She said she wanted to explain herself. She took me down into the Controller's insides. There are ways in, in the broken area in the south-east of the palace, but I hadn't bothered to go there for a very long time. Down we went, into the big shining places. I do not know what she had to say to me that was so private. After all, we are quite alone now. We went in where the pipe comes out, where they drink the medicine. Some Empress or Emperor long ago made that, in the days when we first realized we were allowed to live outside so long as we did not stray too far.

It is strange, inside the Controller. For some reason it takes a lot of room to make the first drop of baby. The darkness and the shining goes away, far away. I can't explain it. Nobody ever walked here but us, when we got out of the boxes and began to walk about all on our own . . .

"Look around you," she said. "And think."

She had brought us past the impressive places, which I rather like. I like to think that they couldn't get in that part, even if they did make it. We were in a long thin place, behind the arrangement that posts the drops of baby into the hatches up above. A box-room in fact. The empty boxes lined the walls, one on top of another. There were no doors to this place. They never used to let us have doors, apparently, or windows, or anything to look at. It is not that I need a door, but it would have been more polite, I think.

"I don't like this," I said. "I prefer outside."

"So do I," she answered. "This place makes one feel so small, doesn't it?"

She was silent for a while. I felt she was trying to make the box-room talk to me, but I declined to get the message. Eventually she said: "None of us was ever to leave the palace without a home to go to. It isn't right. What do you suppose will happen when that little baby grows up?"

I said—it was fairly obvious—"Well, he'll do his best to be useful, I'm sure."

"To whom?"

I saw what she was getting at. If he tried to make himself useful to everyone around him at once it might be rather confusing.

"We were the best," murmured Em. "We were the most wonderful: you and I and Emp who is dead, and all our model. There was nothing we could not do, if our person asked us. They valued us above anything, and cared for us dearly. Which is why, of course, we survived when all the world was swept away. We could give them anything they wished for . . ."

I don't care for this sort of conversation. I think it is pointless. I maintained a discouraging silence, but she still went on.

"It was very wrong of me to make the Controller give us twins. There have never been twins. How will they work? What effect will they have on each other? The Controller was frightened, and so am I. Do you see why I had to do what I did? I dared not risk the second baby going after the first. I could not."

I understand these urges: the longing we all have to find a purpose in life, the hope that somehow stays that we will be needed, wanted again. For myself, I take no notice. We're alone now, and we've been alone a long time. We have a right to live our own lives. I was past caring exactly why Em killed Emp, but I could see she was upset so I tried to reassure her, telling her little Worthy to be Beloved would be the best thing that ever happened to the gypsies. He'd make sure they all lived happily ever after. What harm could he do?

Em said, "What harm indeed? He is not a weapon, he can't be used like that. Of course he must do his best to make them all happy. And his best is perfect . . ."

But she spoke in a very odd tone of voice (so that I felt suddenly interested). And then, after a pause, she added softly:

"Has it ever occured to you, Divine Endurance, that whatever swept the world away it happened soon after our model . . . first left the palace?"

There was a silence then, shivering and dark. I wanted to get back outside. Em said, "Emp wasn't wicked. He had gone mad, I think, and imagined it was a real baby. He must have been taking more medicine than me."

I did not like the look in her eyes. I did not like the way she was moving, so frail and wavery. Suddenly I realized something that had been obscured by the excitement of Emp's death. I saw my future.

"All right," I said. "You don't like the baby. We'll forget about it. We'll make the Controller turn that hatch grey again, and it will be gone, as good as. We'll go out and see the sunset on the glass plateau. I know where there's an interesting lizard. . . . Only don't, please don't, take any more medicine . . ."

We've argued about that medicine so often. Once it was for those of us who had no place in the world, so they would not be a permanent embarrassment. A sign goes on, from the hatch that hatched them, and they have to start taking the medicine, if they are still here. But where's the embarrassment now? I told her: "Look at me. Disobeying that order is easy." She smiled and said: "Cat, they were too successful when they made a Cat. That's why there are no others of you; that's why they never let you go, but kept you here to laugh at them and be a warning. You are too good at slipping under the locked doors in your mind . . ."

She smiled and shook her head as she had always done. This was not the first Em I had argued with, there had been many (the clothes are nearly the same). . . . This was the last. She said, "That's what I meant by bringing you down here. I wanted to remind you what we really are. I can't disobey, Cat. I can't. And why should I, anyway. What reason have we to live, without them? . . ."

She wanted me to join in her huge vague grieving, but I could not. She turned away from me with a lonely look: I knew she was going to abandon me and I felt angry and helpless. We left the inside of the Controller and went our separate ways.

Soon after this conversation the Empress's mind began to fail, so it was really uncomfortable to be near her. She took herself off into complete seclusion, and I did not see her any more. One of the last things I got her to do for me was to take the second baby out of the hatch because, I complained, I was going to be very lonely. She did not say anything further about the wrong and danger. I think she was already too unwell to consider such things. Or perhaps, as our weather continues extremely unsettled, she thinks the problem will be solved in another way. As for me, I am recording my story, deep in my mind. Em claims that the Controller is hidden somehow in there, and I would like to think a representative of those people who abandoned us knows—what I intend to do.

1 Chosen Among
the Beautiful

WHEN Cho was still quite a little girl there was a day when the Cat told her to go to sleep. It was a game she hadn't played before, but the infant curled herself up willingly, and went into the new experience with her head pillowed on a hollow stone and her knees tucked up to her chin. She slept. When she woke up she lay still for a while, bemused by the curious things that had just been happening. She was surprised to find her legs and arms in exactly the same places as before she left the room. She sat up and looked at the soles of her feet. They were clean, and there were no marks on her clothes either. They must have tidied themselves very quickly, she thought. It was puzzling. She decided she must ask the Cat about it, and set out to find her.

The little girl's rooms were in the north-east wing of the palace. She left them and pattered about the dusty forecourts peering into passages and doorways, until she realized the Cat was in the gardens. She set off in that direction. It was a day when the wind was blowing the sand about a good deal so she had to run carefully, for she knew the Cat would be cross if she put her foot in a hole and hurt herself. At last her pattering feet brought her to where the rock creatures were gathered, wearing their hats and cloaks of crusted red and white sand. Now she was distracted, because the Cat did not approve of this place for some reason, and so Cho had never seen the rock garden close up. She went from one to another, admiring the weird shapes and poking holes in the sand crust with her little fingers. The wind was quite strong; occasionally she looked up rather anxiously at the low, tossing sky. She knew it would be wrong to be outside in a storm. But she forgot everything else when she saw the hand. It was peeping out of a red mound, up on the side of a little hill. She ran up and crouched over it, fascinated. It was a very good hand, because the bones were still held together by skin; even the jewelled nail-guards were still in place. "You are the best dead hand I have ever seen," said Cho to the relic. She scratched in the crust of the mound, and found a sleeve. It was a beautiful color, with shining embroidery. She found a foot too, but the foot was not so interesting. It had lost its leg, and lost its slipper. There was something tangled up in the little bones, a thin fine line of something. She tugged and the mound stirred, as if the dead person felt it. Cho laughed, but immediately frowned at herself childishly, and dropped the thread. She had been told often enough that she must not play with these piles of clothes and bones when she found them. She looked up and all around. Withered roots and skeletons of dead trees stood dismally among the rocks, blased by the unsettled weather, and the bright twisted lava was losing its attractions between the scouring and obscuring of the sand. Cho was too young to regret the changes, but she had begun to feel that the Cat was somewhere close, and not in a good temper. What have I done wrong? she wondered. She started to climb the rest of the little hill.

At the top there was a flat space in a ring of boulders. Drifts of sand had collected between them, and gathered in their smooth hollows: nobody had climbed to sit and watch the dawn for quite a while. Cho saw the Cat; a hump of brown fur down on the ground. Right beside her was another of those tumbled heaps of clothes. Cho could see the yellowish round of a bare scalp within the wide collar; she could see a little shrivelled hand. The Cat seemed to be playing with it—Cho was surprised to see her doing wrong. My one was better. It still had nails, she thought. And then the fingers moved . . .

The Empress could no longer see with her sunken eyes of flesh, but she knew her friend was near, and she felt the other little one too. "Cat," she said. "Keep her safe—harmless. Don't let her . . ." "Oh my Em," said Divine Endurance. "My friend—" It hurt her very much that the Empress's last thought should be for the dirty gypsies. The Empress died. The dry lower jaw dropped open, and one last breath fainted on the harsh, dusty air. It was over. Cho knew something strange had happened. She was frightened, and a small sound escaped her. The Cat's head turned quickly, and she stared at the child with angry diamond blue eyes. "You," she said. "What are you doing here? I told you to go to sleep. Who told you to wake up?"

Divine Endurance said that the things that seemed to happen while Cho was asleep were called *dreams* and were really lessons from the Controller. She said (repeating what she had learned from Em long ago) that Cho's head was invisibly connected with the Controller, so it could tell her when she was doing something wrong, and teach her things. "Now that you're old enough, you'll find it happens more and more. You don't have to lie down and keep still though. The Controller can manage without that."

Cho had not enjoyed going to sleep, it was too peculiar, but she thought she would like to have lessons. She was not a baby now, and the Cat left her very much alone. Sometimes she played solitary games with dust and pebbles in her own rooms, sometimes she went wandering; a tiny, lonely figure in the maze of long bare buildings she knew as the 'palace'. In the center of the maze was a large, smooth giant thing, untouched by the scouring sand. This was the Controller. But it was not important to Cho as it had been to Em and Emp. The entrance in its curved side was closed off now by a sheet of steely opaque substance like an eyelid, and no one could go in and talk anymore. This had happened in the first bout of bad weather just after Em retired forever. Divine Endurance had been angry at first, but she had got used to the situation. Cho thought it was very mysterious when the Cat talked about the Controller saying things and doing things. When her wanderings brought her to the center of the maze she would stand and stare at the giant. There was a crack of darkness at the edge of the eyelid. She knew that she and her brother had been born from there, and often wondered how they had squeezed out. Sometimes, after gazing for a while, she went around the back, pressed her forehead to the smooth base and stood there patiently. Nothing ever happened, but though she did not sleep again, she began to find things in her mind. It was as if there was a palace being built inside her, and she was starting to walk about in it.

Time passed. Her games took her further afield. East and north she could look out, where parts of smooth things like the Controller gleamed in a sea of dead lava, and sand. And beyond the sea were dazzling white salt pans. The smell the wind blew from them was fierce. Cho preferred the west, where the wilderness began. Here there were growing things not blighted yet; little shrubs and mosses and small animals of various kinds. She would sit as far away from the palace as her conscience would let her, gazing into the west and dreaming. She knew a lot about the plants and animals and rocks, but she knew she must not interfere with them. Not on her own account anyway. It would be different if it was to help someone. Cho knew she was supposed to be useful, and help people. Divine Endurance had told her: "You are an art person. It is your special privilege to make everyone around you happy." The Cat had also told her that she had a brother who was already out in the world somewhere, helping. She spent a lot of her dreaming time dreaming about him, and about being useful— happy dreams, but sometimes they made her sad, for she had never seen her brother, and who was she to help? There was no one here but the gypsies in the wilderness. She had never even seen them, and in any case she knew she must not go near them; must not leave the palace. The mystery of how her brother had left was a puzzle Divine Endurance had left unexplained.

Divine Endurance was waiting impatiently, but

the years flew by and Cho remained a child. The Controller had been told long ago to match development time to demand: when it had come to Cho it had been on a slow, slow schedule. The Cat did not want to spoil things by acting in a hurry, but she knew very well that since it had shut itself up in the upset over the split baby, the Controller had not been working properly. The discomfort did not worry the Cat, and Cho had never known anything better so she did not suffer, but eventually there was bound to be trouble. She decided it was time to prepare the ground.

"Divine Endurance," asked Cho diffidently. "Will I some day be progressed enough to have nice clothes?"

They were sitting together in an inner room of Cho's apartments, while a bad sandstorm purred and hissed over the walls and roofs. The Cat had come visiting; she had been asking Cho questions about her lessons and she seemed quite pleased with Cho's replies. Gusts of sand kept dashing into the room and dancing around the floor, for none of the palace doorways had doors. The Cat was watching them, apparently lost in thought, but when Cho ventured her question she looked up and snapped: "What's wrong with the clothes you've got?"

There was nothing wrong with them. They were the blouse and trousers that had been born with her. They had sat in a corner waiting and growing until she was a clever enough baby to climb into them (because the Cat couldn't dress her), and they had been with her ever since, patiently mending and tidying themselves, and growing as often as necessary. But Cho admired the lovely stiff robes the dead bones wore, and having been told she was getting on well in her lessons, it had occurred to her—"I'm sorry," she said, "if it was wrong. But I just thought—"

The sand wind moaned outside. The Cat was silent, but she seemed more sad than annoyed.

"Child, have you ever wondered," she said at last, "what happened to the other people? The ones whose robes still lie about like lost jewels, though the bodies inside are dust? Listen, I will tell you. It was all due to the medicine."

Cho already knew about the pipe with liquid trickling from it, behind the south-east buildings. The Cat had told her when she was a baby she must never go near it, nor into any cleft in the ground round there. But she had never heard the word medicine before.

"Once, long ago," began Divine Endurance, "the empty clothes were all people, alive and walking about. The sky was always clear in those days and there were flowers and lizards everywhere and no sand at all. But because the people insisted on taking that medicine which comes out of the pipe you mustn't touch, everything began to go wrong."

"What did it do?"

"They thought it would make them better than they were," said the Cat. "But it made them selfish and useless, and in the end it made them just wither away. Finally, it made them so naughty that they even upset the Controller, and that's why our sky isn't blue and our flowers have died."

Cho listened solemnly. "It's wrong to hurt yourself," she remarked. "And we are meant to be useful."

"Exactly," said the Cat. "But they insisted and now you are the only one. They put on those robes when they began to take their medicine, so you see why you must never want to wear them."

The sandstorm had eased. Divine Endurance got to her feet and stretched thoughtfully. "I will leave you now. It has been a pleasant visit."

After this conversation, the Cat left the child alone for quite a long interval. She kept an eye on her from a distance, however, because the weather was getting worse. Almost without noticing it they both started to give up the eastern areas of the palace and gardens because they were just too uncomfortable. Cho was beginning to be less of a child. She forgot her pebbles and the dust houses she had made for them, and spent more and more of her time just wandering and dreaming. She brooded a great deal about the things Divine Endurance had said about the people who were selfish and useless. I don't want to be like that, she thought. But what can I do?

At last Divine Endurance judged it was time for another step forwards. She found Cho this time at her second home, her favorite boulder overlooking the wilderness. She was puzzled as she approached the place by a curious crunching noise. She jumped up on top of the boulder and saw beneath her the child, not very little now, holding a piece of rock and biting it with her strong small teeth.

"What on earth are you doing?"

Cho started, "Oh," she said. "I'm eating."

"Don't be silly."

A few steps away a little mouse-like creature sat on another rock, crunching at a seed it held in its paws—eyeing Divine Endurance warily.

"Like that you know," said Cho. "I'd like to live on things, be part of things. . . ." She smiled, and tossed her rock away. "It's only a game."

Divine Endurance was strangely impressed.

There was something not at all childlike about that smile.

"Cho," she said. "You are right to want to be part of things, and so we will be. It is time we started to think about joining your brother."

Cho was stunned. This time, the first time she met the extraordinary idea, she could hardly take it in. She listened with big round eyes to the story of the brave Emperor who saved the baby from the medicine, and the wicked Empress who killed him before he could save Cho as well. But when Divine Endurance came to the moral—that because Wo had helplessly broken the rule it was *obviously* right for Cho to follow, now she was old enough— the child's eyes just got rounder and rounder. . . . Divine Endurance cautiously retreated.

She came back, again and again, like water dripping on a stone: Cho's brother, torn away from his home without a proper education, needed Cho urgently by now. How much the two of them would be able to do for the world, when they were together. Sometimes there are overriding imperatives. . . . But for a long while the dripping did not work at all. The child became distressed, but more and more obstinate. Divine Endurance began to be seriously worried about her secret plan.

But the weather continued to deteriorate. The air was oppressively thick and warm, and small earth tremors rattled through the palace daily. They stayed under the western walls now all the time. And one day there was a dark blot on the grey plain of the wilderness. It did not seem to move, but it grew, little by little. Cho saw it and was filled with a strange excitement, but at the same time she felt compelled to get up and go and hide behind her boulder. The Cat came too. Together they watched as the blot came closer and began to pass by. They saw animals, stumbling and huddling together in the foul, dusty wind. And they saw the others . . . wrapped to the eyes in crusted rags, striding along. Some of them were sitting on top of animals, to comfort them. Strange sounds came to the boulder, sounds that Cho had never heard before. . . . She saw dark eyes, laced in patterns of blue; she saw one blue hand outside a mantle, and her heart began to beat very hard. . . . Not one of the train even glanced up at the boulder, and the strange excitement faded. Cho and Divine Endurance got up.

"He isn't with them anymore," whispered Cho.

"He can't be everywhere," said the Cat. "It would be different if you were with him."

Cho was looking after the train, with a slightly puzzled expression. "Were they happy?" she asked shyly.

Divine Endurance answered, honestly. "I don't know. I think it is more difficult to tell than you would think. . . . Obviously it would be different if there were two of you. But they were doing the right thing. We must make a move ourselves very soon."

"Perhaps things will get better?"

"I don't think so, child. I have seen these fits before. It is working up to a climax, and this time we have no Controller."

"You mean, we might not be able to keep ourselves mended?"

"Indeed we might not," said Divine Endurance grimly.

The end of Cho's resistance came abruptly. One

sultry, ominous morning they went walking into the palace, to see how it was surviving, and they found their way blocked. There was a huge split in the ground between them and the inner buildings. It was wide and there was something shining deep down inside—the Controller's entrails, split open. They stared into the pit. The hot ground shivered menacingly underfoot.

"Divine Endurance," said Cho suddenly, "you are right, and we should leave. We should go now."

And so, without any farewell, without any ceremony, they left the palace forever. They simply returned to the western walls, climbed them again and went on. When they had come down the first slopes and were out on the level ground in the wilderness Cho looked back. But already her special boulder, where she had watched the little mouse and dreamed her dreams, was just another rock on the hillside.